Tales I carry with me

BARNEY ROBERTS

McPHEE GRIBBLE/PENGUIN BOOKS

McPhee Gribble Publishers Pty Ltd
66 Cecil Street
Fitzroy, Victoria, 3065, Australia

Penguin Books Australia Ltd,
487 Maroondah Highway, P.O. Box 257
Ringwood, Victoria, 3134, Australia
Penguin Books Ltd,
Harmondsworth, Middlesex, England
Penguin Books,
40 West 23rd Street, New York, N.Y. 10010, U.S.A.
Penguin Books Canada Ltd,
2801 John Street, Markham, Ontario, Canada L3R 1B4
Penguin Books (N.Z.) Ltd,
182-190 Wairau Road, Auckland 10, New Zealand

First published by McPhee Gribble Publishers
in association with Penguin Books Australia 1988
Copyright © Barney Roberts, 1988

Typeset in Goudy by Bookset, Melbourne
Made and printed in Australia by
The Book Printer

National Library of Australia
Cataloguing-in-Publication data

Roberts, Barney, 1920–
Tales I carry with me.
ISBN 0 14 011701 6.
I. Title.
A823'.3

McPhee Gribble's creative writing programme is assisted by the Literature
Board of the Australia Council.

To all my grandchildren
and their beautiful parents

Acknowledgements

'Goodbye Jasper' and 'The Landman and The Seaman' were published in FAW Tasmanian Anthologies 1978, 1983; 'Pianist or Poet' published in the *Mercury*, 1985, commended Henry Savery Award; 'Bert', 'No Escape' and 'The Optimist' (previously entitled 'The Orchardist'), were published in the *Eaglehawk Rolf Boldrewood Short Story Award Book*, 1974, 1979, 1984; 'Kelly and the Turk' and 'Charlie and the Bonus' were published in the *Dossier of Tasmanian Writers*; 'Pyramid of Blocks' was published in the *Advocate*, Prize winner *Advocate* FAW Award; and 'The Interview' was published in *Quadrant*, Second prize winner Australian Society of Authors/The *Australian* Short Story Competition.

McPHEE GRIBBLE/PENGUIN BOOKS

TALES I CARRY WITH ME

Barney Roberts was born in Flowerdale, Tasmania, in 1920. Apart from the period he spent in the A.I.F. and as a prisoner of war in Germany 1940–45, he has lived in Flowerdale all his life either as a farmer or in his Bush House as a writer. This is his seventh book. The others include two books of poetry, *The Phantom Boy* and *Stones in the Cephissus*, his P.O.W. memoirs, *A Kind of Cattle*, for which he won the New South Wales Premier's Literary Award Special Award for the International Year of Peace in 1986, and, most recently, a collection of short stories, *Where's Morning Gone?*

CONTENTS

Still here I carry my old delicious burdens,
I carry them, men and women,
    I carry them with me wherever I go,
I swear it is impossible for me to get rid of them,
I am filled with them,
    and I will fill them in return.

Walt Whitman, 'Song of the open road'

KELLY AND THE TURK

Kelly Harmen was born in a tent a few kilometres west of Leonora. His father and mother had lived there on the red sand, amongst the spinifex and mallee, searching for that big, golden nugget, which would take them out of the hot hell-land they hated.

They had arrived from Ireland two years before and followed the rush from Kalgoorlie to Leonora and finally, on the advice of a dying prospector, moved out to a claim some distance from town.

Young Kelly was born when his father was on one of his occasional drinking sprees. He had arrived back at the tent one night to find the new baby lying on the floor in the tent, with the umbilical cord attached to the warm but dead mother, sprawled on her back, with her hands still clutching two fistfulls of red sand.

The father washed and wrapped up the child and took it to a woman he knew at the Sons of Gwalia mine.

Kelly's father disappeared. Some said he had walked out into the desert to die. Some said he had joined the Light Horse brigade which had left to fight the Boers in South Africa. Once, it had been reported, he had been seen with a group of Aborigines who had come into Kokabindie Station for food.

The baby was sick and weak for months and Mrs Harmen nursed it through crisis after crisis. One day an Aboriginal woman brought her a herb mixture and immediately the child started to thrive. 'The little fella is going to live,' Mick Harmen said.

By the time he was six months old, Kelly was a fat, contented child, always smiling, and a favourite with the four Harmen children. The youngest, Merv, was ten years old.

It was not until he was four that the Harmens realized that the boy was mentally retarded. His limbs were short and thick, his big head was joined to a broad back by a short neck. 'A real wrastler,' Mick said. 'Even now, he's as strong as a bloomin' bullock.' He was. And he grew stronger with the years.

Kelly was excused from attending school after spending four years in class one.

Mick made a wheelbarrow for the boy and from then on Kelly and his barrow were a part of the scene around town. Always he was taking something somewhere. Bill Hunnibell, the draper, began using Kelly to transport goods which had arrived at the depot from Kalgoorlie or Perth. Other shopkeepers followed and by the time Kelly was fourteen he was responsible for delivering most of the goods from the depot to the shops.

Kelly couldn't read but he learned to go, as the baker's horse did, by instinct.

Merv Harmen, who ran the depot, organized the local carpenter to build an extra-large barrow. A red sign was painted on the side: 'Kelly's Transport'. Merv watched with pleasure the first time Kelly saw his new barrow. He walked around it, smiling, inspecting every detail. He lifted the front end and spun the iron wheel. He touched the red lettering with his finger. 'Kelly's Transport,' Merv said, pointing to the words.

'Kelly's Transport. I'll be able to go now, Merv.'

He spat on his hands, hooked on to the handles and sped off in a wide circle around the yard. 'Good,' he said dropping the legs, letting it slide to a stop. 'Get on, Merv,' he said. Merv grinned and limping over to the barrow, sat on the front board with his feet braced against the axle-sleeve.

Kelly lifted the handles high, with his fists up near his shoulders. 'Go!' he said, and fairly flew around the yard for five laps before skidding to a stop. 'You an' me'll go in a wheelbarrer race, Merv,' he panted.

Merv laughed. 'I'll need bloody goggles, if you go at that pace.'

'How about we both wear bloody goggles, Merv. We'll bloody frash 'em.'

'Well, don't go practising when you've got a load on, you'll lose your parcels.'

'No fear. Won't drop no parcels. Never dropped no parcels yet, have I, Merv?'

'No doubt about you, Kelly. Come on, bring your barrow round to the back and we'll load you up.'

Kelly stood up straight and saluted. 'Yes, sergeant.' Merv's brother, Tas, had taught him how to salute when he was home on his final leave before embarking for Egypt. 'When's Tas comin' home to see my new barrer, Merv?' as they loaded the parcels.

'Be a while yet, I reckon.'

'He said he wouldn't be long.'

Merv didn't answer. The family had not heard from Tas for weeks, and stories were coming back about the slaughter at Gallipoli.

'He said he wouldn't be long. Why don't he come? What's he doin'?'

'He's fighting.'

'What's he fighting for?'

'It's the Germans. We've got to fight them – them and the Turks.'

3

'What's the Turks?'

'They're bad people. They're what Tas has gone to fight.'

'What's up wiv 'em?'

'Aw, don't ask me, Kelly. All I know is they're bad and we've got to fight them. I'd go myself if it wasn't for this foot.'

Kelly looked sadly down at Merv's twisted foot which had been broken in a rock fall years ago. 'If I'd been a bit older I would'ave come down an' lifted that rock off your foot.'

Merv grinned. Good old Kelly; he'd already forgotten about Tas and the Turks, at least for the moment. 'I reckon you would'ave too. As Dad always says: you're as strong as a bloomin' bullock.'

'I'll show you how strong I am, Merv,' and lay down on his back, his knees up, his hands, palms up, on the ground by his shoulders. 'Come on, get on, Merv.'

'Gawd,' Merv said, 'we'll never get any work done the way we're going.' He limped over to place his feet firmly on Kelly's hands.

'Right,' Kelly said. 'One.' He lifted Merv straight up and down again. 'Two – three!' A quick heave and Merv was catapulted through the air, over the top of Kelly's knees, to land far out in front of him. Merv stumbled on his gammy leg and fell sideways.

Kelly was beside him in a moment, helping him up. 'I didn't hurt your foot did I, Merv?'

Merv looked at the big face, and laughed. 'Of course you didn't. I just forgot for the moment that one leg was shorter than the other.'

'I wouldn't want to hurt you, Merv.'

'You great, soft coot. I can't think of nothing you'd ever want to hurt. Your trouble is you're getting stronger than you think.'

'Kelly's strong as a bloomin' bullick,' his face like a morning sun.

4

Kelly went off down the street, nodding and smiling to everyone. Shopkeepers came out to inspect the new barrow and the load which Merv had stacked in the order it would come off. 'What's the matter with you, Kelly?' Bill Hunnibell said. 'You still haven't got the parcel of trousers I'm waiting for. Everybody will be running around with no pants on if you don't bring them soon.'

Kelly bent forwards, laughing, crossing his hands over his privates. 'We'd look rum then, wouldn't we, Mr Hunnibell.'

From shop to shop he trundled his barrow until there was only one heavy crate left, which Merv had placed against the front board. 'That big one is for Lizzie Beamish,' Bart Temple, the chemist, said. 'It looks heavy.'

'Kelly carry. No worry, Mr Temple.'

He went back up the street and stopped before Lizzie Beamish's novelty shop. He pressed his hands and his nose against the glass, picking out the items, one by one: ornaments, pictures, dolls, coloured bottles, vases, ribbons, lace.

'What are you going to buy today?' Lizzie Beamish was smiling down at him from her doorway.

She was a middle-aged woman who lived on her own, at the back of her shop. Everything about her shone: the gay cotton dress, which clothed her short, comfortable figure, was, as usual, neat and fresh; her face a soft pink as if it had been scrubbed with sandsoap; her black hair, particularly this morning, Kelly noticed, sparkled in the sun. But he looked away quickly. There was always something in Lizzie Beamish's friendly, brown eyes that scared him a little. There was no need for him to answer as they both knew that he only bought things twice a year: once for his mum's birthday and once for the family at Christmas time.

'What's the crate?' Lizzie asked. 'You forgot to deliver one.'

'That's for you.' Kelly said.

She walked over to look. 'So it is. I know. It'd be my new

camp oven. Good, good, good!'

Kelly grinned. She looked so pleased, almost as if he had given it to her. 'I'll carry it,' he said. Effortlessly, he picked up the crate and followed her through the shop, down the narrow passage into the kitchen.

'Put it there, please, Kelly. I'll get a hammer or something to take the top off.'

Kelly placed a knee on one board and gripping another with both hands, pulled. The long nail creaked and gave. One after another he ripped off the boards. She was smiling at him. 'Such strength.'

'Kelly, strong as a bloomin' bullick.'

'Oh yes.' She stood directly in front of him and very close. They were about the same height, their bodies the same width. Kelly's eyes were held by hers. 'Such strength,' she whispered. His nostrils dilated like a frightened horse. She touched her hands on his shoulders, leaned forward and kissed his cheek. 'Thank you, Kelly.'

He reached up and clamped a hand over his cheek, turned and rushed out, down the passage, through the shop, out on to the street. He collided with a passer-by. 'Watch out, you stupid bastard.' Kelly hesitated long enough to recognize a stranger, snatched up his wheelbarrow and clattered full speed back to the depot.

'Still practising,' Merv greeted him, then saw his face. 'What's the matter, cobber, somebody go crook at you?'

Kelly said nothing. 'Why don't you park your big barrow in the garage and take your little one to pick up the bottles?' Kelly stared at his friend, his brother, and without a word did what Merv had suggested.

He moved off slowly down past the shops, keeping on the opposite side from Lizzie Beamish's, down past the big gum at the end of the street. He would go first to Harry's place. The old man was always pleased to see him. 'That's the system,' Harry would say, 'always like to see the place clean and tidy.'

The place was a single room, black-iron shanty, well off the road in a thicket of smoke grey mulga and mallee gums.

Everybody knew that Harry had money stacked away. Some thought he was worth a fortune. Some thought he couldn't have much left as he had been living there for years earning nothing. Always he had given Kelly twopence for carting away his empties.

Kelly turned off the road on to the sand track. He stopped, listening, his head cocked to one side. He left the barrow and went quietly along the track. A crashing and the sound of an angry voice caused him to creep cautiously through the bushes. A horse, with the reins thrown over a broken bough was standing quietly.

He sneaked up to the doorway of the shack, his mind trying to grasp what was happening. Harry was on the floor, one arm held up trying to protect a face that was badly cut and bleeding. A man, with his back to Kelly, was holding a stockwhip, the short handle in his left hand, the right holding a length of the whip which he brought down again and again on the old man. 'Where's the money, you bastard? Where is it?'

Kelly struggled to understand. This one must be one of the bad men Tas had gone off to fight. He was the same man he had seen in the street outside Lizzie's shop. He was a Turk. That was it. 'Turk!' he screamed.

The man swung around. The lash whipped across Kelly's face. The handle came down hard against his right ear. He knew all he had to do was to get the man in his arms and crush him – *Kelly's as strong as a bloomin' bullick* – the whip lashed at him again and again – *as strong as a bullick* – the handle cut at him. Kelly's arms were wide, his legs shuffled forwards, backing the man into the corner – a savage, slashing, lashing, cursing – Kelly knew he had him. His arms were closing – clawing, closing. The handle came down, again and again, but weaker now at such close quarters.

7

Kelly didn't care any more. His hands were creeping up his wrists, pressing, crushing this thing in his arms.

He wanted to see Harry, but there was something wrong with his eyes. Or was it the floor he was looking at? Or this thing he held tight in his arms?

Harry staggered up the road for help.

When Merv came he saw the horse standing quietly, resting its near hind leg. Kelly's arms came away quite easily. The thing he was holding rolled a half-turn away from him.

'Kelly,' Merv said. 'Kelly, cobber.'

The puffed and broken face smiled. 'Merv, tell Tas I got a bloody Turk.'

THE OPTIMIST

'Come on in, Harry. You're here about the meeting? I've been telling Jack he's got to go.' All the time she was shepherding him into the room she was keeping one eye on the flies. With that last bit of sun hundreds of them had gathered in the back porch.

Jack Ballantyne only ever half listened to Harry. He thought he was a yaffler. He supposed he liked him all right; he was good-natured, and certainly loyal to the Ballantynes, always had been, but his endless opinions on everything bored him. Jack had a thing about people who couldn't bear silence. If someone came to help in the packing shed, as often as not they'd bring a radio with them and the music and advertisements would be blaring all day. In town it made him cross to see youngsters running around with plugs in their ears, listening to some programme or other. It didn't worry Madge.

Jack knew about the meeting, you couldn't help but know; every orchardist in the valley had been aware of it for weeks.

'We want everybody there,' Harry was saying.

'That's right,' Madge agreed.

'If we don't fight for our rights, nobody else will. We don't want fancy prices. A fair return for our work is what we're after.'

'They don't seem to want our fruit.' Jack didn't know why or even who *they* were. He only knew he and Madge had grown quality apples for, must be, forty years; some years the prices were good, some years not so good, but they had always got by – till now.

'I'll tell you why they don't,' Harry said. But Jack still didn't know after Harry had finished. He had picked up bits about South Africa, doing away with the middleman, getting rid of the Minister for Agriculture. 'I'll call fer you then, Jack, in about an hour.'

Madge watched him, holding the door open. Farmers never seemed to know how to finish off a conversation; the same, she thought, when they were on the phone. 'In or out, Harry,' she said finally, 'you're letting the flies in.' She had seen a dozen or more pass his head.

'Sorry, Madge. See you, Jack.'

He left, leaving the woman moving about the room on her short thick legs, slapping at flies, unnecessarily violent in her killing, and the man, sitting silently, except for the drumming of his fingers on the table. 'I don't think I want to go to their meeting,' he said.

'Their meeting. It's as much yours as theirs. Anyway, you as good as told him you'd go.' And added another corpse to the small black mound in her open palm.

He wondered whether she would ever stop. She had to be moving, doing something; except mealtimes, but then only long enough to eat before she was taking his plate to wash it. A cup of tea she would have on the run, leave it on the sink, or the bench where it'd get cold, pour a bit out, put a bit more hot in, a few sips and leave it again. 'You ought to meditate, Mum,' Jenny, their oldest daughter, had said when she was last home. 'Twenty minutes in the morning, twenty minutes at night.' And Madge had replied, 'Where d'you think I'd find the twenty minuteses? I'll leave that for those with time on their hands.'

'That's thirteen I've got that Harry let in. Of course you've got to go, Jack. As Harry said, it's numbers they want.'

'I suppose.' Build up the numbers – about all the use he'd be.

She turned on the tap and washed the dead flies down the sink. 'Get changed, Jack, while I get you something to eat.' Her voice was soft. It was what held them together, always had done; they were like one person with two minds: argue things out, but always leave off before anyone got too angry.

This was different, this what the papers called the 'fruit crisis'. It seemed it was becoming a personal problem. For a few years they had been on the perimeter, watching the occasional farmer go under. They had hung on, buying less, drawing on their small reserves until there was no more to draw on; Madge knew, she did the books. Jack knew too, but he wouldn't face up to it. He would get outside, in amongst his trees, where he could forget that anything had changed; where he wouldn't allow himself to think that 'it' (what had happened to the Larks and the Hills and the Gammages) could ever happen to them.

He watched her lift the lid of a saucepan to let off the smell of onions. The backs of her legs, apart from the knotted veins, blue against the skin, were brown from years of exposure to wind and rain. She must have humped thousands of cases over the years.

He came back, dressed in his navy blue suit, shiny on the seat and shoulders. She straightened up his collar. 'That's better. Now sit and eat.'

The only sound in the room was the slurp of his eating. She had long since learned to take him a bit at a time.

Jack Ballantyne was never one for meetings, but according to Harry every orchardist in the valley would be there tonight, at least those who were left would be; there were a lot who had taken advantage of the Government's tree-pull programme and sowed down their few acres with grass. The owners had bought cattle when the prices were high, fed them for a couple of years, sold at a loss, and gone off looking for a job. A few of the wealthier ones had been able to buy out a couple of neighbours, but in most cases the farms were small and over-capitalized with equipment and sheds only good for orcharding. The total market price was barely sufficient to buy a modest suburban home. The buyers were mostly city businessmen who wanted a weekend hobby farm.

Jack was interested in what these people were doing with their properties; and critical too, like all the locals. 'What's the bookie doin'?' he asked Harry as they drove past what, until two years ago, was, for three generations, an orchard owned by the Jones family. For the locals, the dip in the road below the property would always be known as Jones's Gully.

'He's putting in a track for his trotters,' Harry said. 'This is what makes me mad: they're all the same, these bastards — dirty great houses, swimming pools, trotting tracks, you name it. On top o' that some of 'em supply the supermarket with cut-price fruit.'

'It's no good getting mad,' Jack said.

'Well, do you reckon it's right? These blokes have all got another job. Take that doctor bloke down at Massey's, you go to him for ten minutes in town an' he'll charge you three times as much as he'll pay for a full hour picking. You reckon that's good enough?'

'Yeah. But anyone can pick apples.'

'You reckon?'

'Well, it don't take that long to learn.'

'What about pruning?'

'That's different.'

'Yeah, well, he wanted to cut me down on that.'

'Did he?'

'I told him to stick his apple trees. I got a real kick out of that. You should have seen his face. In the finish he got old Knocker t' do 'em. Talk about a mess.'

Jack Ballantyne let him rave on. Something about the time of day with the sun new gone – except for the few places like the top of Bailey's Hill – had swung his mind back years to one evening when he and Ted Bailey had sat on the bank at the edge of the bush. It was only a few weeks after their fathers had been drowned on a fishing trip from Dover to Cape Bruny. He and Ted were nineteen at the time, and as only sons had taken on the responsibility of the orchards. The view that he saw now was not a lot different from the one he and Ted would have seen then: the neat, orderly rows of trees, houses, packing sheds, green flats sprinkled with tea-tree and rubbish, the river and the black bush on the other side of the bay. It was all pretty much as he remembered it.

Ted had been killed up the desert. They had been sitting on a bit of a hill near Bardia, cussing the sand; Ted talking about the times they used to sit on the hill back home. He had stopped in the middle of a sentence and when Jack had looked at him he saw him slowly fall sideways, with a trickle of blood running from a small hole in his head. Then, as when his father had died, as always when some disaster happened, Jack Ballantyne was able to absorb the shock. The battle was with himself. Inside himself. Some thought he was heartless. Or dumb. He wouldn't have argued.

They pulled up near the hall behind a string of cars. 'There's a crowd all right,' Harry said with obvious satisfaction. 'That's what we want.' He left Jack and hurried over to talk with one of the members of the organizing committee. Jack went into the hall and sat in the back row. He watched the seats filling in front of him. Several politicians, with carefully prepared smiles, waved and nodded to anyone who looked their way as they walked the length of the hall. But it was not yet time for them to sit. They would talk to anyone, to each other if necessary, until everybody in the hall knew they were present.

Jack listened to the various speakers telling everyone what they already knew. Then, at last, the Minister. He was short and fat with a bald head which sparkled under the glare of a dangling globe. He talked without interruption. He quoted unintelligible figures: costs and prices, the effect of the industry on the balance of trade, something about the gross national product, the necessity for farmers to market their own product. 'Our Government is sympathetic –'

Jack Ballantyne was lost. Everyone to their own trade. He knew about growing fruit – anyone in the district would agree to that – he was not interested in the marketing side; leave that to someone a lot smarter than him: that politician perhaps. He looked at the man's hands, short, fat fingers spread wide in a gesture of appeal, and wondered if the man had ever picked an apple. But what did it matter? He wished he had not come. He still had to turn the irrigation off when he got home.

The Minister was saying how he understood and sympathized with the orchardists' predicament.

'Balls!'

He ignored the remark. 'Some of you must inevitably leave the industry. We shall help you to do just that.'

'What about a bit of help to stay in?'

'We intend to do that too. We have plans under consideration at the moment. We ask you to be patient.'

'It's easy to be patient on your salary. Would you be game to buy an orchard?'

'It's his sort what does: for a weekend cottage and a hobby farm.'

There was a roar of laughter. The chairman held up his hands.

'Look, the Government knows what you people are put-

14

ting up with. We need you and your industry. I promise . . .'

'We're sick of your fancy promises. We want action!'

And so it went, from uproar to uproar, until finally a motion from the body of the hall called for an action committee to be formed.

Jack Ballantyne waited outside. The pointers of the cross were almost vertical. Somewhere, a long way off, a bullfrog kept dropping a double note. The crowd was emptying out of the hall. At home, their families would be waiting to hear of a miracle.

Harry talked most of the way home, rehearsing and embroidering the interjections and the snippets of speeches which appealed to him. Jack was relieved to be dropped at his gate. Madge was waiting for him. She poured him a cup of tea, then sat and demanded answers to her questions.

'In other words, he told you nothing new,' she said at last.

'That's about it.'

'Then we'd better start thinking about selling before everyone else does.'

'Selling?'

'We can't go on the way we're going.'

'We can hold on as long as anyone.'

'You don't do the accounts, Jack. You just don't know.'

'It can't be that bad.'

'Can't it just. How would you feel walking into a shop with the backside out of your trousers and knowing you can't get a new pair because there's no more money? Every time I go to town I dread the thought of having an accident and being taken to hospital. What would the nurses think? Where do you think we buy our clothes? We don't. If you used your eyes you'd realize that everything we wear we bought years ago. It's all been mended and mended and mended. I'd give anything for a new pair of pants. They call it a free country; it's free all right: free to starve; free to work for eighty hours a week; free to go on a holiday, except we

15

can't afford the bus fare into the city. But there's one thing we are free to do and that's to sell out and get out, and I say the sooner the better.'

He noticed her bosom was heaving, which was a sign. She rarely got so stroppy. 'Where would we go? What would we do?'

'That old house next door to Jenny could still be for sale. We should get enough for this to buy that, surely. Anyway they said they'd train us for another job.'

'Train us! I'm too old to be trained for anything. I'm an orchardist. And that's all I'm good for.'

'We've got to live.'

'We'll still live. We've lived through hard times before.'

'We'll live behind bars, if we go on the way we are going.' She stood up and reached across the table for his cup. 'Do you want another?'

'No thanks. I'll go and turn the water off.'

'Then don't let the moths in as you go out. And there's another thing, every night you walk right down to the dam to turn the water off: what about that fancy automatic gadget you've been talking about, couple of years now, must be?'

'I'll get round to it.'

'Huh! Too late now. I don't know why you turn it on at all, just so you can have more fruit to rot.'

Outside he stood for a few minutes waiting for his eyes to adjust to the night. There was a feel about the place. And a smell. He breathed in deeply. His eyes saw past the dark shadows of the trees, the rows and rows of apple trees that, in winter when the branches stood stiff and bare, lined up in squares and diamonds; trees that rested for a time then burst with new-life buds and pink and white flowers, so that the whole countryside was a land of scent and colour.

He walked down the track with the stars blinking over his shoulders, the trees, sentries, on either side of him. There was the clack of sprinklers and the hiss of water on leaves.

He could almost see the apples growing. It would be one of the best crops ever.

The ground was soft under his feet.

He stepped under an unpruned Prince Alfred which his grandfather had put in, a graft from the original tree planted by Mrs Parsons at Blackfish Creek. He touched the rough bark with his hands; a communion with three, no, four generations of fruitgrowers. 'It could be, if we leave here, you have grown your last apple.' What was it his grandfather had told him? 1868 was the year the Duke of Edinburgh had come to Tasmania. It was the same year Mrs Parson's seedling tree had born its first fruit.

At the pumphouse by the dam he turned off the motor. Except for the leaves dripping it was quiet. Was Madge right?

He picked up a stone and under-armed it into the dam. The stars danced. He sat on the grass, his arms curled around his knees, and leaned forward, letting his forehead rest on the back of a hand.

He had no brain for thinking things out. Ideas, solutions slipped out of his grasp just as he felt he had the answers. There was something crazy happening. Fair enough, if you can't sell your apples, don't grow any; but why should people die, millions, so they reckon, and millions of apples rot on the ground? Crazy. All he could do was follow a line. When the time comes you'll get it, like Ted Bailey did, fair between the eyes.

He picked up another stone and stood up. This time he threw it so there was a sharp thunk; the surface of the water barely rippled.

A cow not far away bellowed.

He walked back through the trees. One time or another he had touched every branch on every tree in the orchard.

A small animal scuttered across the track in front of him. It was a bandicoot, he knew by the way it moved.

He stopped on the track by the last row of trees. A brush

possum barked. The kitchen light was still on. A yellow light fell in a path across the yard and leaned up against the packing shed, where the spouting hung.

He could see her sitting at the table, facing the window. He knew she couldn't see him standing there in the shadow. On her left were socks, neatly folded, tucked inside each other, in pairs, as he would find them in his drawer. One sock was pulled down over her left fist, and with her other hand she plunged the long darning needle carelessly, carefully, filling up the hole with crossed threads of wool.

Again he heard the rustling in the bushes, but closer now. His eyes followed the sound, followed the small animal which came into the strip of light, scenting at the ground, advancing erratically towards the man, who stood perfectly still, waiting. The bandicoot stopped, to sniff at his boot. Jack Ballantyne bent down until he was resting his forearms on his knees. Even in the dim light, he could see it was a scabby mangy brute, probably loaded with ticks. It began sniffing at the sock above his boot. 'You're sick, Bandy. Or old. Old more'n likely. Had your day.' He flipped it away with the back of his hand. It rolled over, kicked awkwardly, regained its feet and stumbled off in the direction it was pointing, back into the long grass. He stood then, hearing the shuffling movements grow fainter. The thing was lost. It had probably spent its life hereabouts – and was lost. Poor coot.

His feet crunched on the gravel. At the back door he stuffed his boots in the cupboard, the same as he had done every night since he was married. 'You can always tell the kind of people in a house after one look at their back step,' she had said that first day.

'Come on,' she said. 'You've had enough for one day. You must be tired.' She noticed his shoulders were hunched forward. He suddenly looked old.

'I do feel a bit tired,' he said. 'There was a bandicoot right

18

there by the back door. It's a wonder the old dog – I was thinking about that house next to Jenn's, there's a bit o' land out the back –'

She was on her feet, sweeping the mound of mending back into the basket. 'There's one thing about mending, you never seem to get to the bottom of it.' There was the hint of a smile on her face.

UNCLE CLARRIE IS DEAD

For thirty years Jason had been going to Claxford to spend his holidays with Uncle Clarrie. Nothing much had changed, unless the changes had come so slowly he hadn't noticed.

Henry (after thirty years Jason realized that he still didn't know Henry's surname) was still the mailman and prattled non-stop, but not objectionably, for the twenty-five kilometres from the Junction Hotel on the highway to Claxford township.

The voice, the engine noises, and the scutter of stones as the vehicle bounced along the metal road, were all a part of the coming back; a part of the release from city living. So too, the climb up through the rainforest, where, in places, the giant myrtles reached out to touch above the road.

Jason knew the road well enough to anticipate the dips, the twists, the racing creeks, the tunnel of light, which led at last to the top of the range. From there, for a few short moments before dropping steeply down through the bush to the plains, he could glimpse the wide circle of fertile farming country with all its roads spoking into the cluster of shops and houses which was Claxford.

Thirty years! Now it may all be ending. Mrs Hite's telegram had brought him back this time, out of season: *Uncle Clarrie very low Stop Asking for you Stop Come at once Stop Mrs Hite*

He may already be dead. Henry hadn't heard. So be it. Uncle Clarrie had taught Jason to accept. If he were dead, there were other paths.

Uncle Clarrie was dead.

Mrs Hite shouted out the news even before they had stopped at the garage-cum-post office. 'You're too late, Mr Jason,' she yelled, sucking back the teeth, which would otherwise have burst onto the cement step. Then, as the engine cut, her voice affected sanctimony: 'He's passed on, poor man. At least you'll be here for the funeral.' She opened the passenger door. 'I'll run you up there, if you would like to see him. He's been laid out and Rudi is going up this afternoon with the box. I've got the car here ready.'

'I'll walk, Mrs Hite. Thank you just the same.'

'Come on, I'll run you up. It's a long . . .'

'He said he'd walk,' the garageman said abruptly, smarting still, that his wife had got in first with the news.

'Yes, you walk if you want to,' Henry said. He had his problems with the postmistress, too.

'Thanks, Mrs Hite,' Jason had no wish to offend, 'but I think I would sooner walk.'

'It has been a time, I can tell you,' she said, accepting, as best she was able, his decision.

It seemed unreal that Uncle Clarrie would not be there to meet him as usual with his cheery 'Jason, me boy, good to see you'.

'They all call me Uncle Clarrie,' he had said that first time.

Jason had regained consciousness in a strange house

– house? – hut, with one big room; table, bed, stool, everything split or round, straight out of the bush. Smoked and warm and no wonder, with the huge stone fireplace and logs blazing.

Uncle Clarrie was leaning over the fire to hook the handle of a kerosene tin on to a wire. He had snow white hair which had been slashed at with scissors, leaving a series of horizontal overhangs. His grey, short-sleeved flannel showed brown, muscular biceps, incongruous on skinny arms. He had turned quickly when he heard Jason move, advancing to peer at the round, wide eyes of the patient. Unbelieving, the two men had stared at each other. 'So you're awake.' It was almost an accusation. Or an expression of impatience, ingratitude even, that it had taken so long for the man to regain consciousness.

As he lay recovering on the stranger's bed, Jason wondered, as he had wondered so often since, what it was that controlled the destinies of people. He knew why he had felt compelled, in the first place, to go off on his own, to cross the wild Wadell Mountains. His father had done it years before, and from childhood Jason had had the desire to copy him.

Others had said, 'You're mad. It's too rough. You'll never make it.' But eventually he had found himself standing on the crag that overlooked the Claxford Valley. It was the end of a mission. Hurrying, laughing, slithering down rocky slopes, tripping, clutching at a piece of brush (that Uncle Clarrie told him afterwards, had to be prised from his fingers), falling, tumbling, over and over – then nothing. Until he had wakened in the hut.

Jason stopped halfway up the road which ended at Uncle Clarrie's hut on the edge of the bush. His breath came in short, sharp pants, causing him to realize just how old he was, how many years he had been coming to this place. He turned to look over the valley, to the town and beyond, where the white, ribbon road climbed up to the pass.

So. He was back again. This time, apart from the death of his friend, there was a difference. It was late autumn, not mid-summer. The colours were softer. Not far away, a man, or a woman (the tractor cabin distorted the figure inside), was ploughing a paddock, exposing the grey, alluvial flat soil. Nearer, a herd of golden Jersey cows grazing on a paddock of Algerian oats, many on their knees, were reaching as far as possible beneath a single electric wire. A boy on a trailbike with open exhaust, burst out of the bush on Jason's left and dodged, erratically, across a stump-strewn paddock to an unpainted weatherboard farmhouse that appeared to be sinking gradually into the ground. Nearby, three men were working on what looked like the foundations of a new one.

Claxford, after thirty years of little change, was on the move.

Jason, tired and depressed when he reached the hut, walked into the room, darker than he remembered it, without the fire which Uncle Clarrie had always managed to keep alive. He stood, waiting for his eyes to adjust.

He frowned at the figure lying on the bunk, moved over to it, touched the cheeks with the tips of his fingers and shuddered. The skin was cold.

He threw a blanket over the body and busied himself lighting a fire, a huge fire, which threw light into corners.

Jason felt better after he had drunk several mugs of tea. He hadn't thought to bring any food with him, but he found some stale bread and some rancid butter. A wallaby tail, which stank, he threw on the fire.

He moved about the room, touching familiar things, greased and shiny from handling. He remembered how they had sat talking after the night meal, the flames lighting up arms and faces. Yet he could remember nothing much of what had been said. Things about the bush? It didn't matter much. There had been no reading of books, no listening to music, just the sound of the wind, the animals, the night birds. There were times when they would leave the door ajar, and the brush possums, and sometimes a native cat, would come in to accept the crusts the men tossed to them – the way the firelight flashed in their eyes and burnished the tips of fur.

The welcome, the quietness, the old man's talk, the log fire, to go to sleep watching the flames, were all things he had found himself looking forward to each year as his annual holidays approached.

He had always experienced the same winding-down of built-up tensions, the joys of relaxing. He was finding it more difficult each year to go back to his job in the city.

When it came time for him to leave, it had shocked him at first to realize that Uncle Clarrie had had enough of his company. There were no handshakes, no turning to wave, just a friendly, if offhand, 'Righto, son, see you sometime.' And a turning away.

Jason was aware, now that the old man was dead, how this two or three weeks in a year had come to be an essential part of his life. He knew now it was at an end. Uncle Clarrie had been allowed to stay where he was on sufferance for his lifetime, by the owner of the forest. The hut was worthless and would soon decay or be destroyed.

There would be no coming back to Claxton. Jason would find a place: a small hut in the bush somewhere, to live as Uncle Clarrie had taught him how. He had no dependants and enough money to see him through the rest of his days.

When Rudi arrived with the big, meaty, red-faced youth to, as Rudi put it, 'box 'im up', Jason sat watching.

'You was a good mate of Uncle Clarrie's, wasn't yer?' Rudi said, displaying an easy expertness for his job. 'Relation?'

'No, just a good friend.'

'Knocks you about a bit. Always does. Some more 'an others. A good ol' bloke. Never 'armed nobody. Not much of 'im though.' They lifted him into the coffin. 'Natural causes, o'course. The funeral's fixed fer two o'clock tomorrow, at the church – C of E – there was a bit of an argument about who would get 'im, but we reckoned 'e probably was. Usually are, his sort. That right?'

'Yes,' Jason said, not knowing, not caring.

'The C of Es are quickerer than most,' Rudi said. 'The Romans are quick enough at the cemetery, but they mess about a bit in the church. The Gospellers! They can take upwards o'two hours by the time a few of 'em 'as a go – an' what with the weather. You'll be there, o'course. It's a bit lucky, I've 'ad one of them new mechanical jiggers for lowerin' the coffin for a couple of weeks now, but nobody's carked it lately.'

They picked up their burden and moved out the door. In a few moments Rudi was back. 'Never like to mention this sort o' thing when there's been a death in the family, like – not as if –'

'Oh, I'm sorry,' Jason said, pulling his wallet from his pocket, 'Could I pay for everything now? I'll be returning home, straight after the funeral.'

He watched the car move slowly down the hill, then walked out into the bush, leaving the door as he had found it, wide open.

He'd have three or four hours for one last look around before night; nothing too strenuous, just poke about a few of the old places where they used to go. In the gully, bauera vines had already started to close off the tracks, leaving the well-worn animal pads below. On many of the others on the higher land, uprooted trees, which Uncle Clarrie would normally have cleared with his axe, lay spread across the paths. It was as if the old man had been dead for months.

When he returned it was already dusk. There was a mist settling on the flats. He'd have to make do with toast and tea tonight. And in the morning.

He tossed the dregs of his third cup of tea in the fire and put what was left of the bread and butter back in the safe. He threw on a few logs, filling the room with light. One after the other he took three blankets off the top bunk, shook them outside, then laid them on Uncle Clarrie's bunk. He had no qualms about sleeping where a dead body had lain a few hours before.

He stopped in the middle of the room. Unconsciously, he glanced back to the bed, as if the old man might be there. The room seemed suddenly empty without him, without his occasional bit of talk. It was strange that a man could leave so little behind. There were a few clothes, a shirt and a pair of trousers which he had obviously purchased not long before, an old pair of boots. But apart from the necessary things there was nothing much: no books, no firearms, no bits and pieces that anyone would normally collect.

If Uncle Clarrie had left a message anywhere, Jason knew where he would find it. He swept the bits of rubbish from one of the hearth stones and carefully inserted the poker under one corner. He lifted the stone and took out a wooden box.

There was no message, no will, only notes which he let flutter in a heap on the floor: fifties, twenties, tens, twos. Carefully he counted out the exact amount that he had given to Rudi, folded and tucked it into his inside pocket. He'd fix up with the parson after the funeral; it wouldn't be much.

Jason looked at the pile of notes. He knew that as soon as he moved out the scavengers would be in. He'd give them something to hunt for. He put a ten dollar note in the box and replaced it and the stone. He filled the crack with dust, scooped up the rest of the notes and threw them on the fire. He threw another couple of logs on and without undressing lay on the bunk. He watched the flames and the patterns of the burning coals.

Sleep came easily and without warning. He was wakened twice during the night by possums clambering over him.

When he had breakfasted the following morning, Jason decided he would look for the spot where Uncle Clarrie had found him. It was a long walk but there was little else for him to do.

He was sure, because of the steep escarpment covered with bushes, that he had eventually found the place, yet nothing was as he remembered it. It would be easy for him to believe that the whole episode had been a dream or that it had all happened in some other bush.

When he returned to the hut he was surprised to find it was so late. Hungry after his walk, he ate the last crust of bread and swallowed half a billy of scalding tea. He left the mess of blankets, the used plates and mugs, left the fire smouldering and the door propped open, and walked down the hill without a backward glance.

Uncle Clarrie was dead.

CHARLIE AND THE BONUS

Charlie Platt was tall and thin with acne scars on his face and neck. He was reliable, even good at his job on the factory floor as a maintenance man. But who wouldn't be, after twenty years? Same job, same routine; well almost: eight years ago there had been an updating on the Thunder Line, which had considerably reduced the noise factor by a number of decibels. It had taken Charlie no more than five weeks to adjust to the new routine; and what is five weeks out of twenty years?

Intelligent? Hardly. Charlie had the intelligence of a good cow dog which had been rounding up the same herd for ever; a pattern of behaviour which time and experience had made predictable and reasonably proficient.

In retrospect he could hardly have been blamed for the accident. Most likely it was a frayed belt: a strand of cord which had snatched the wrench from his grasp and forced his hand into the pulley. Either that, or an uncharacteristic lapse in his concentration.

Charlie had been offsiding all his twenty years at the factory for Gerry Edgers.

Gerry was bright. The certificate to prove it was framed

and hanging on the wall above the bar in his loungeroom. Twenty-five years ago Gerry had won the State Apprentice of the Year Award. There had been many examples since of his intelligence and initiative; and it was not just recognized by the Company. He had periodically resisted approaches to take on responsible positions: shop steward, union boss, parliament even. 'You're a sitter, Gerry,' the party boss had said. But Gerry was one of those rare individuals, fortunate enough to be content with his lot.

There were those few, possibly provoked by jealousy, who regarded him as 'a bloody scrounger'. Gerry would have been the first to admit that he had, at times, been able to make use of certain bits and pieces of machinery which would otherwise have gone to the dump, but 'a bloody scrounger', he didn't care for that much; his *Cassells* said: 'scrounge [etym. doubtful] v.t. To pilfer, to cadge', which put him off that bit more.

Gerry was right. It took brains and an understanding of human nature to get these odd things past the gate. 'You'd better let us have a look what you got there, Gerry,' the gatekeeper had said one evening, and when Gerry opened his coat a black cat flew out and ran back around the corner of the factory. 'Bugger him, my wife wanted a black cat particular,' and Gerry ran off after it. When he returned, a few minutes later, he was hugging this thing under his coat. 'Got him this time,' he said triumphantly.

'Then keep a holt on him,' the gatekeeper had said. 'Bloody cats. I don't like 'em.' Some said the cat had turned into a new one-horse motor; but that was rumour.

Then the wheelbarrows! For three nights Gerry had come out with a company barrow piled high with shavings. 'They're for me raspberries. They tell me there's nothing like shavings for raspberries.' But the gatekeeper was a suspicious type. As Gerry remarked one day, 'His job 'ud learn him to be suspicious of everything and everyone. No wonder his wife left him', which was a fact. Each day the gatekeeper searched down through the shavings and found nothing. 'You don't think I'd pinch anything, do you, George?' Gerry stopped after three nights; he reckoned he had enough shavings to do the raspberries *and* to light the fire through the winter.

Charlie and Gerry were mates. Always. They had started school together, got married the same year, lived in the same suburb, and both worked at the Pulp. Always. An unlikely pair, a lot would think: one tall and skinny and a bit – some people thought, some even said it – a bit retarded; the other short, fat, and – no doubt about it – bright.

Gerry and Charlie were on night shift; they had been through the nightly procedure, the regurgitation of partly digested news of the day: local sporting, political, police-court, births, deaths, break-ups of marriage, general scandal and rumour. It was about time for one of them to have a sleep when the accident happened.

Charlie had done it hundreds of times, without being caught. Regulations stated that certain adjustments should only be carried out when the power was turned off. There was a warning notice on the wall, which no one ever read. Regulations were for beginners. Charlie Platt wasn't a beginner. It could have been because it was the last day of their night shift, or that Charlie had been doing about four hours a day on another job – that he was physically tired and lacked judgement. But Charlie knew it must have been the frayed belt that caused it. What he knew for certain was that there was a sharp, searing pain that came from his right hand and beat like a jackhammer in his brain.

It had happened once before to a man who could show a hand with half a thumb and four stumpy fingers to prove it.

Gerry Edgers heard the wrench clatter on the steel floor and looked over to see his mate swing his right hand up under his left armpit, then move over to turn off the switch.

'Leave it on,' Gerry shouted and ran to him. 'We won't turn it off,' he repeated, 'or we'll have old Alec down here to see what's up. Is it bad?'

'I think I cut my bloody hand off,' Charlie said.

'Let's have a look, mate.'

Charlie held out his hand and the blood ran on to the floor.

'Your hand's still there. It's only a bit of a cut.' Gerry picked up an oil rag from the bench, wiped the blood off the floor and put the rag over the wound.

'I'd better go an' get it fixed.'

'You can't. You know what day it is. The boys 'ud murder you.'

'Bugger 'em. I got t'get it fixed.'

'Think of the boys. Let's wash it and see how bad it is first.'

They went into the washroom. Gerry filled the basin with warm water and pressed Charlie's hand into it. 'Jesus,' Charlie said. The water changed colour to a dark red.

'My old man used to swear by metho,' Gerry said, 'for anything – metho or kero.'

'Probably what killed the bastard.' Charlie spoke bitterly.

'Let's have a look at it, mate.'

The belt had run up the side of the palm, from the wrist to the end of the little finger. 'Waggle your little finger,' Gerry said. Charlie waggled and it moved. 'There you go, mate. She ain't bad. Nothin's broke. She's just a bit of a graze.'

'Bit of a graze! Look at it! It'll need fifty fuckin' stitches!'

'My old man used to say a cut always looks worse than it is. Cover it up to stop the dirt gettin' in and let nature take its course, he used to say.'

'Gawd! That's a foot long and an inch deep!' (Charlie decided long ago he could never think in metric no matter what.)

'Think of the boys,' said Gerry.

31

In spite of the raw wound Charlie was relieved to see his hand was still intact. 'I've got to do something, Gerry,' he said.

Charlie had really forgotten until Gerry reminded him. If they got through the day accident free it would beat the previous record of sixty-nine days by one, and the management had promised a special bonus for all employees. If Charlie had treatment and had time off for an accident on the job, the blokes would all lose their bonus; as simple as that.

From the moment Gerry heard the wrench crash on the floor and saw Charlie swing his hand up under his armpit, his brain was wrestling with every possibility: how to stop his mate reporting an injury received at work – how to keep the bonus in other words. Then he saw the answer. 'I've got an idea,' he said. 'We'll rip the bottom off your shirt and bind it up a bit, then you can go along to Alec, keeping your hand hid in your pocket, and ask him if you can go home and turn your stove off . . .'

'The bloody stove ain't on.'

'Listen, mate. I'm tellin' you my idea. You go and see old Alec and tell him you've got to go home to turn your stove off . . .'

'An' I'm tellin' you it . . .'

'Fer Christ sake, listen, can't you. Your wife's gone away to stay with her mother . . .'

'But she bloody ain't.'

'Let's imagine she has. She's gone away to stay with her mother for the night, and before she went she left a batch of bread in the oven and told . . .'

'But she don't bake bloody bread. She couldn't bake bloody bread if she tried. She can't even fuckin' cook.'

'Aw, shut up and listen, will you,' a little impatiently. 'She left this bread in the oven and told you to turn it off before you went to work and you forgot . . .'

'But I didn't bloody forget. She didn't bloody tell me, because she don't bake bloody bread, and anyway she 'ad a row with her old woman, so she wouldn't be goin' there.'

'Charlie,' Gerry said (in a quiet voice, like sometimes he used talking to his kid, when he kept asking *why*), 'just let's imagine all those things I told you was true, and you told all those things to Alec, and asked him if you could duck back home and turn the stove off, and you'd be back again in five minutes.'

'Aw, Christ! What's all this tryin' to prove? Me bloody hand's nearly cut off and you're tellin' me to go 'ome an' turn a bloody stove off, which ain't on, because it's supposed to be burnin' some bloody bread me wife ain't baked any'ow. An' then on top o' that you say t'come racin' back 'ere.'

Gerry smiled at his friend. 'You're gradually getting the hang of it, mate. Now listen, careful. After you've been home and turned the stove off, you walk out to your car and get in. Now listen to this. When you get in your car, you're feeling down the side with your right hand for your seat belt and without thinking you grab the door with your left hand and slam it, hard. You don't realize it but your right hand is up against the doorpost, and when you slam the door it cuts it right down the side.'

'You're bloody mad, y' bastard. D'you think I'm likely to jam me 'and in the bloody door after the way it is?'

Gerry was still grinning. 'You don't really have to do it at all, mate.'

'Then what did y'say I did for? I'm buggered if I know what's come over you.'

'What I'm saying, mate, is you don't really do it. You don't really turn the stove off. You don't really jam your hand in the door.'

'You'll be telling me I don't really have to go 'ome at all, in a minute.'

'That's right, mate.'

'An' I don't really say nothin' to Alec.'

'Charlie,' Gerry said, 'you've got it all right, except you do tell Alec, and then as soon as you come back, you rush in and find Alec and tell him what you've done.'

'But you just said, I didn't bloody do it at all.'

'You still tell him you did, but you don't.'

'I see,' said Charlie sarcastically, 'I tell Alec I did, but I don't.'

Gerry took a deep breath. (It was harder than he had imagined.) 'Now, let's get this straight, Charlie, cobber,' (that word 'cobber', thrown in like that, only for real matey occasions. He'd have to use all his diplomatic tricks, he'd seen Charlie this way before, once he got piggy there was no way –) 'you tell Alec everything we decided to tell him.'

'I didn't decide to tell 'im bloody nothin'.'

Gerry put up both his hands just as he had seen the priest do before he blessed someone. 'All right, mate,' quietly, 'everything I said to tell him; you know, about the stove, and your wife, and the bread, and that, and then you go out and drive your car around the block a couple of times and after about five minutes you take your shirt off your hand and drive back. When you get out of the car you hit the side of your crook hand up against the doorpost, to smear a bit of blood on it, like, and to make your hand bleed better. That's when you come racing in to tell Alec what's happened. Now do you get me?'

Charlie looked at his friend, in silence for a bit, then like an early morning sun peeping over Round Hill lighting up the place, you could see the understanding getting the better of him. He smiled. 'What you're tryin' to tell me is I've got to tell Alec all this that I'm goin' to do, but don't, just so I can make out I didn't bloody do it 'ere, but did it in the door of the bloody car.'

'That's right, mate.'

'An' this way we won't lose the bloody bonus.'

'That's right, Charlie, cobber. Now you've got it.'

'Well you better bloody tell us again just what I gotta do.'

'All right, mate,' said Gerry, 'now what you've got to do is this . . .'

THE BURYING

The funeral was set for Sunday morning eleven am, which allowed enough time between morning and afternoon services, to go home for dinner. Berry and Hope (members of AFDA, for ethical and personal service) couldn't fit it in on the Friday – 'a bad day anyway, clashes with the auction at Bridgeton' – 'and Saturday the cricket semi is on, Sunday there should be a good rollup.'

The four of us were standing at one end of the grave; Roger's wife, who incidentally had only met her father-in-law on her wedding day, was holding a lace handkerchief and periodically dabbing at her dry eyes, but carefully, not to smudge the white eyeshadow, which had replaced the vivid green of yesterday. Roger had only been back to Tasmania once since he left for Sydney fifteen years before, and that time he and Casey had had a big row. He was a stranger to the town and to most people at the funeral.

Roger was tall, blond, good-looking and over-weight. On the other hand, I was small, dark and insignificant, except that on this day I was the one everybody knew. I still played football and cricket for the town firsts, and, for the record at least, I was the youngest son of the deceased. Aware of my lack of height, I had carefully chosen my position on the edge of the mound of earth to raise it closer to that of my brother's.

Had I ever wanted a public funeral? The answer is a big NO.

All arrangements were taken out of my hands when Roger came down from Sydney. Arrangements had always been taken out of my hands by Roger.

It had been easier to let him have his way. And there were ways of getting what you wanted, without appearing to, but this time, when I had been determined not to give in, I had lost again.

Roger said, 'We must give him a proper send-off. It's what the old man would have wanted.' Which was utter hypocrisy, of course. I said so and we both knew it. But I think we both knew too that Roger would have his way; hadn't he always? I had conceded, ungraciously, taking no part in the organization of the funeral or the party which was to follow, before Roger and his wife returned to Sydney.

The solid walnut coffin (Roger's decision) with the fancy decoration and chrome handles, waiting for its final lowering into the grave, shone brilliantly in the morning sun. Inside was Casey Middleby.

I could visualize Casey's face as I had found him, dead in his bed, four mornings before. I had been profoundly shocked, not by the death, but by the expression which I had not seen for years it seemed. I had become used to seeing him maudlin drunk, contumelious, or servile, and lately, always forbidding. In death, all that had gone. A splash of sun had caught his face; the mouth was relaxed, the eyes almost smiling. Obviously he had died at peace with himself. I had touched the bare arm which lay on the cover and with the back of my hand the cold forehead.

In the kitchen I found Gwen and the two children arguing about something or other. She had looked up as I entered, 'Is he getting up?' (Once it had been 'Dad', now always 'he'.) Her voice was flat, tired. What could I expect? She had a husband (that's me), who refused to face up to her problem

37

of what to do with an irresponsible and objectionable father-in-law; even the kids were becoming obstreperous. On week-days I had been pleased to escape, to leave her with her frustrations, her problems. I knew it couldn't go on indefinitely. Someday, my castle of dreams would collapse; she would become fed up with the situation, and with me. I was powerless to avoid what seemed inevitable. Then suddenly the cause of our problems was dead. Yet all I could answer was 'No', and continue on into the garden. Now was not the time to tell the children.

It seemed an hour later when Gwen found me on my knees, carefully pulling weeds from a row of seedling carrots. 'I'm sorry,' she said. 'I didn't realize.' She rested a hand on my shoulder. I covered it with mine, fingers red from the dirt. 'It's funny,' I had said, 'last night was the first time since Mum left – what's that, twenty years ago or more – that I've heard him mention her. He said: "I wonder what happened to Joan? I hope she's happy".'

As seems typical of a Methodist funeral in our town, the Minister was eulogizing Casey Middleby's early life: his brilliant scholastic record, his sporting ability, his achievement in rowing and the tragic accident which had forced him to withdraw from the Olympic rowing squad, his years as head-master of the state school.

I was making a cursory count of those present and in doing so realized that I was centre stage. As I glanced from person to person and eyes met, I guessed it was necessary for them that their presence be noticed and acknowledged. There was Hec Cowman, the captain of our footy club who put me nineteenth man for the last match of the season. I didn't expect to see him, or Larrie Smithfield ('Dog' his nickname, and he was one), I wonder did he come because he felt guilty? And Tip Porter of course; he skited he'd never missed a funeral in forty-one years. Tip was the retired town carrier, started off with horse and float before the war, graduated to a FX ute which he crashed in '75, and retired. I wonder do a lot of them feel that I would be offended if I knew that they hadn't attended? I had counted sixty heads and knew there would be as many again in the half circle behind me. Most of them would want to file past, shake our hands and mumble condolences after the service.

I kept looking past the Minister's shoulder to the cliff that rose steeply from the sea, about three hundred metres up to the plateau. After last night's deluge (luckily it fell after the cricket semi which we won by three runs in the last over of the day – a thrilling finish. I realize suddenly there's Happy Whackful winking at me – Hap really won the game for us, went in last man with three to get, opened his shoulders and got six off the first ball – I give him a sly wink back) the black rock was gleaming where the sun struck it. Two people, splashes of colour, in the distance, were working their way up the face.

I knew intimately the best track up from the small sandy beach, where the waves pounded in the easterly weather. On countless weekends I had rowed my dinghy across the bay and spent hours climbing or just poking about the rocks. On the beach in recent times with Gwen and the children we were a family, just the four of us. To see Gwen, temporarily free from her worries, playing chasings with the children, splashing and being splashed, laughing – I felt like howling for what we'd lost, for what we had to go back to.

There were the times, when I was a youngster, when Roger and I had gone with Casey. A part of his programme was to train us (me, lightweight skulls or cox) to be King's Cup rowers: an attempt to salvage something from his own shattered hopes. Once he had been hailed as the best stroke prospect for the Berlin Olympics in 1936, until his shoulder had been smashed in a car accident when returning from a party after his selection.

His disability had put him out of competitive rowing, but after years, married and with two sons, (Roger, the oldest, strong and athletic), his ambitions had been rekindled.

I still remember vividly, and with resentment, the early morning dashes to the river, the swimming, rowing, climbing, running. At school holiday breaks Casey organized our daily programme, watched over our diet, forbad most social activities, bullied us into believing, as he did, that someday one or both of us would be champions.

Some said it was the result of his accident, these sudden changes of mood from passionate enthusiasm to fits of dejection. After a spell of drinking, he would invariably be left in a state of maudlin melancholia. While he had never hit either of us, I had known plenty of occasions when he raged and shouted uncontrollably.

The atmosphere at home had become insufferable. Roger, then a strong lad of sixteen, made surreptitious visits to his girlfriend, arriving home in the early hours of the morning, and gossip had it that Mum had a lover who called sometimes in the daytime, and at nights on those odd occasions when Casey took us on what he called a training camp. Gossip has a habit of eventually reaching the ear of the concerned party. So it was with Casey. Several days before the event, Casey made a point of telling Mum that he and the boys would be spending the night camped on the beach at the foot of the cape, ready for a first-light climb to the top.

All went to plan. In the evening he gave us a strenuous training session, a meal, then early to bed. He must have waited until we were asleep before returning to find, as he had feared, Mum in bed with a man from a neighbouring town. He put the chain on the gate, let himself into the house, picked up Roger's Don Bradman 4-Star Special and flung open the bedroom door. The man, who he recognized as Randolf Sparkling (Randy for short, who Mum had often employed to fix problems in the TV, the washing machine, the fridge and a powerpoint or two), took one look, summed up the situation in the flick of a switch and raced out of the bedroom with only time to snatch up a shirt, collecting a square cut across the arse from Casey's bat.

The two of them evidently made several revolutions of the garden. When we saw it the following morning the garden looked as though Hec Cowman's poddies had spent the night there – beans, peas, rhubarb, artichokes – a real mess. Although the early accounts of the chase over the garden wall with Randy holding a shirt over his front – (Casey must have thrown his clothes out the window because we found them in amongst the tomatoes) – were many and varied, it seems the number of people who actually saw the chase down to the wharf, or at least parts of it, grew from day to day, until it became difficult to find anyone who hadn't seen or heard something. It had ended at the wharf where Randy took to the water, with Casey brandishing the bat and shouting oaths at him until he disappeared into the bushes on the other side of the river.

When Casey arrived back at the house he found Mum had gone too, taking with her a few clothes and things off the top of her dressing table – including the photo of Roger and me she had always kept there. Gone in her little Austin Marina.

And when we searched for it afterwards, we realized she must have taken the Cat Stevens record which she played a lot. I remember once coming home from school early and there was Mum sitting on the stool with her arms folded, her elbows on the bench top and tears on her cheeks, staring at nothing, with the old Cat lamenting: *That's no way to live your life – you allow too much to go by – and that won't do – no – lover I want to have you here by – my side – now don't you run, don't you hide –*

41

By the time Casey recovered from his binge it was general knowledge that Mum had cleared out with Randy, some said to Queensland, some Western Australia, though I don't think anybody really knew anything apart from the fact that they had both left Tasmania. A few days later, Nev Trott, the bookmaker, actually saw them getting on the early morning plane for Melbourne while seeing a friend off at Devonport, and couldn't get home fast enough to pass the word. Strangely, Roger didn't seem concerned; if I said anything he would shrug and say, 'I suppose she'll be back when she gets fed up with Randy'; but I didn't know how to handle the situation: I waited in vain for Casey to talk about her.

It was unreal, as if Mum had never existed; he cooked and cleaned, bought what clothes we needed, and was more considerate than I had known him. It was then that he stepped up our training programme; before, it was strict enough, but after Mum left, it became an obsession. I tried several times to talk about Mum; each time he would respond with some brusque reply like: 'Forget her, she's gone, she's not worth thinking about', until I realized I would have to accept that she had probably gone for good. I was upset, too, that I never had a letter from her, and began in a strange, mixed-up way, to hate her.

The training programme Casey set us left me so tired I found I had no time or energy for anything other than work (at school or training) and sleep. It would have been a common sight for those living on the river frontage to see Casey with his pushbike, stopwatch and loudhailer, riding along the promenade, pacing Roger and me, and yelling advice and encouragement.

But things were going wrong. Two weeks before the State Elimination Trials Roger's times were slowing down. Casey thought he must have pushed him too hard, too soon. He had gone stale: a few days complete rest, then a picnic at the beach, rock climbing if we felt like it, anything, nothing.

But it didn't work. I knew why. Roger had begun revisiting his girlfriend. Several times a week when Casey had gone to bed, Roger would sneak out through the window and return an hour or two before dawn.

I sensed Casey's disappointment and tried even harder. On two occasions I clocked faster times than Roger, which surprised us, and shocked Casey. All the hopes, that he had evidently nursed for years, that Roger was going to restore his pride and liberate him from the sense of failure were being extinguished. Frustration, depression, bewilderment, and the anger, which boiled up unreasonably (and met by his son with the same stubborn silence that Casey was capable of) left him miserable and washed out.

I have a clear memory of one night when Casey apparently was unable to sleep and for some reason, neither was I. Occasionally I think it happens that a sense of some imminent disaster can reach beyond normal confines of logic and reason. I'm sure neither of us had any knowledge of the other's restlessness, until I heard Casey leave his room the first time to go to the toilet, and a little later to boil a jug, I imagined to make the strong black coffee that he often took in times of stress; and later the sound of the opening and shutting of the drink cupboard for whisky.

I pretended I was asleep when I heard him walking towards our room, open the door, and after a moment, turn on the light. I sat up in bed then, looked where he was looking, at Roger's empty bed. 'Where is he? – You know – You have known all the time – Why? – Is it a woman? – A stupid question, of course it is –'

He walked across the room and stood there looking down at the empty bed. He leaned over; this huge bulk of a man leaned over and thumped with fists, which I'm sure had never hit another man, thumped his son's pillow, until at last several small feathers flew up, escaping from the battering.

I sat with arms encircling my knees. Not knowing. Afraid too, of violence, and unprepared for the face which turned to me, with pellets of tears glistening and ridiculous on a stubble of beard; mouth opening and shutting, a stranded fish, gasping, desperate.

I was unprepared, uncertain what to do or how to handle it, when Casey, big, ugly, helpless Casey, with arms out-stretched, collapsed on the bed, clutching at me, holding me, his face pressing into my neck, his wailing chilling me – until words came – and a little sense – nonsense – claiming me as all he had left – as loyal – true – good. He was pressing his cheek into my shoulder. And all I could feel was pity.

When Roger returned, what seemed hours later, with the pale light of morning, a rooster crowing somewhere, answered by another, he didn't notice me sleepless, wide-eyed, watching. He did not see his father lying fully clothed on his bed, staring up, until Roger stood above him. I watched Casey, taller and bulkier, slow-motion move to stand up. No word was spoken. Slowly he turned away and walked from the room.

From that day on it was as if Roger were some casual acquaintance or a boarder. There were no more training sessions. We were left to do as we wished.

I had missed what the Minister had been saying. I saw the undertaker's foot press the lever. I saw the coffin slowly, miraculously, move down into the earth.

The climbers, I noticed, had reached the top of the cliff. They were standing, dark silhouettes against a colourless sky. One figure had an arm thrust out horizontally. Through their eyes, I could see the mountains, the bays, the peninsulas, stretching into the distant haze, a merging of land and sea and sky. I had seen it often. I would see it again and again.

Gwen and I would take the children. The first few times we would go by the track. Then we would tackle the harder way – a bit at a time. I would always remember that first child-climb, the exhilaration, the thrill of achievement, after the uncertainty, the fear. Like so many things. Like life. There's always a cliff to climb. You don't stop with fingers and toes searching for holds to look over your shoulder at the view. That can wait. I heard the crisp earth dropping on the coffin.

For the first time since Casey had died I felt the danger of emotion overwhelming me; not of sadness, but relief, joy almost, that I was free. Free! I would shout it from the cliff top. I was free from the man, I knew now, for certain, was not my father. I *was* Randy's child, as the town had been whispering for years. But I didn't love Randy, I loved Casey, the man who had suffered all those years the knowledge that his wife and his only son were gone from him, that he was left with the son of the man who cuckolded him. Yes, I loved Casey, the man who had nearly wrecked my marriage, who was dead, who was better dead. Happily dead, his face had told me that.

The service was completed. The Minister shook hands and left. A procession of mourners followed; an endless, slow procession of well-wishers, shuffling, with heads bowed, or with words of cheer.

I too would escape.

An elderly woman (for a moment, I thought it was my mother) touched my arm. 'God bless you,' she said. For one short, terrible moment, I thought how I would not, could never refuse to take into our home my own mother – but the moment passed, and Gwen reached up to take my arm.

THE LANDMAN AND THE SEAMAN

Peter doubled the pillow under his head and stared out of the window to wait for the moon. He heard his mother walking about in the kitchen, the clink of cups and saucers. She was making supper.

There was a glow on the horizon where the spit of land ran out into the sea. Mr Kent could be out there on the headland; people said he moved about when the moon was full. Once the boy's mother had screamed in the night. She had seen Mr Kent's face at the window, she said. But his father had found no one. 'I even went down through the boobyallas and looked along the beach,' he said, 'but there was nobody about.'

'I saw him. I saw him. I know I did. I'm afraid of him. He's not normal. What would he do to our boy?'

Through the thin wall, Peter had heard his father soothing her. 'There, steady now, he's a harmless old man; a hermit, likes living alone. He's all right.'

Peter watched the moon's light lightening the sea and the land; its round eye lifting out of the water. A twisted gum laid its shadow on the ground. A grey shadow. Only where the tea-trees were thick and clustered by the creek was it still night. Black by the creek. The sand glistened. Glistened where the water had been.

As he lay staring out of the window at nothing, at every-thing, he saw Mr Kent's eyes, just the eyes in a blurred, bearded face, there on the sea, on the beach, even in the blackness of the tea-trees; the eyes, as he saw them that first time. He had come across Mr Kent kneeling on the grass patch behind the dunes, holding a Pacific gull which had swallowed a bait of some sort, attached to one end of a fishing line, the other end tied to a stone. He had stood watching the man examining the bird, wanting to run, but curious.

'Come here.' Mr Kent had seen him. His eyes were brittle, angry. The boy must do as he was told. 'Did you do this?' Then the eyes softened. 'No. I've seen you often on the beach. You wouldn't do that. What is your name?'

'Peter. Why has it swallowed the string? It's very old, and thin.'

'It isn't old. It's a baby. Someone set a trap for it. It has been here a long time.'

'You mean, someone put food on a hook so that the bird would swallow it?'

'Perhaps not on a hook. I hope not on a hook.'

'What will you do?' The boy was no longer afraid. He knelt beside the man and reached out to touch the bird.

The man had cut the string. 'I'll take it home. Perhaps it will live.'

'Will you feed it?'

'Yes.'

'Can I help you?'

'Yes.'

They had walked along the sand track, Peter hurrying, to keep up with the man's stride. Was it a dream, or had he walked beside this man often before? Wasn't the other man nursing a sick bird? Was it another man? Wasn't it this man, and this bird, and this place? The hut, he knew, would be untidy, but warm and dark.

'Will the gull live?'

Mr Kent looked at him. 'Are you fond of birds, Peter?'

He nodded.

They had said nothing more and walked on to the hut. The man put the bird on the floor. It made no attempt to move, but lay, squatting with its black-tipped bill stretched out in front of it. The boy had stroked the feathers. 'It's soft. It's too soft to die.'

But it did die. When he hurried back the following morning he found Mr Kent working on a new boat. He knew that the bird was dead. 'The bird is dead,' Peter said. Mr Kent looked at him and nodded.

He turned away and walked out to the farthest end of the headland, where the rocks were washed smooth and clean by the seas that sometimes crashed in from the west. 'The bird is dead!' He keened it to the wind.

He stood on the last of the big rocks. The water made slapping noises below him. He looked along the beach. A pacific gull was cruising, five, ten metres above the waves, towards him, coming closer. He stood breathless, still, except for the hair that a light wind swept across his face. He may have been a pinnacle of rock. The bird's huge, hooked bill was bright red, the breast wholly white, the flesh-red eyebrow surrounded the white iris of the eye. The boy felt he could almost touch the bird, it was so close. Without seeming to move its wings, it caught an upward air current, then drifted on down the coast. He watched until the bird was no more than a speck in the distance.

That had all happened some time ago. Peter watched the moonlight sparkling in the waves as they curled and broke on the beach.

'My mother doesn't want me to come here,' Peter said one day.

'Then don't come,' Mr Kent had replied.

Peter had looked at the man, and away. He knew he would come back, again and again. 'People say you live out here because you are afraid. Are you afraid? They say you have done something really bad.'

The man stopped working on the boat and looked at the boy with eyes the colour of the sea. Peter hoped he was not angry. 'No,' Mr Kent said at last, 'I'm not afraid; not here. Do you think I am bad?'

Peter smiled. 'Will you teach me how to build boats?'

The boy stretched out a thin arm on the bed covers. The moon's light touched the skin and the soft hairs. He turned his head and saw the window-bar with its iron latch shadowed on the wall.

I'll watch the shadow move down the wall until it reaches that picture, then I'll go to sleep.

A voice kept calling to him: 'Come down to the sea, Peter.' And he went willingly. They ran together along the sand. 'Follow me,' the man said, and ran out on the water, and the boy followed. 'If you grow tired,' the man said, 'rest on the bird. He will carry you.' He called to the bird and slid on its back. 'Your back is so black now, beautifully, shiny black.'

'I am old now,' the bird said, 'that's why. Rest your head against my neck and you can go to sleep.'

In the morning Peter left the house and walked along the

sand track through the boobyallas. He stopped by the swings to look at a nest of ants that he had been watching the night before. The holes between the cement slabs had been plastered over and there was no sign of a nest. He walked up the sandhill and stood looking out over the sea. Far out on the water a flock of gulls was working. An off-shore wind touched his cheek and tossed the white water on the waves. Small groups of silver gulls walked near the water's edge. Two pacific gulls stood with heads erect, like geese, watching for what the waves might bring in. A molly hawk sat bobbing like a bath toy, its tail high out of the water.

Peter ran down the loose, white sand, twisting his feet, so the sand squeaked; on to the wet, washed sand, that sloped down to the green water. He turned and walked backwards for a while, watching the footprints marching away from him, until the wave hissed up around his ankles. 'Now, when people see those tracks, they'll say, "a man walked up here out of the sea". They'll follow the tracks and find where two people met and went nowhere. Two people met on the beach in the early morning; one came out of the sea, the other came from the land. The Landman said, "I saw you standing on the beach last night. Your skin was the colour of the moon." And the Seaman replied, "I called you but you would not come." "Yes, I did," said the Landman. "Don't you remember, I went to sleep on the bird's back."'

The boy kicked at the water and laughed. He looked about, but he was quite alone. He walked up the wet sand and along where the beach flattened, where the soldier crabs marched by the millions in front of him. 'They are always there,' the boy said, 'ten paces in front of me.' He ran suddenly and the wave of spidery crabs disappeared under him. He stopped, squatting on his heels, still, quiet, watching, listening to the water-dripping, running-water sounds all around him. 'The beach is alive,' he said. 'Millions of tiny sea-creatures live here in the sand.' He saw, suddenly, a worm cast spew up from the flat sand before him, and circle on top of itself, like a live thing. The boy smiled, 'If I wait he'll come up and circle his head around the mouth of his burrow.' But the soldier crabs were on the move again, all around him: at first one, then ten, then hundreds, marching. The boy stood up and laughed, and stamped his foot. And there were suddenly no crabs, only the ones ten paces in front of him.

He ran then, down to the edge of the sea, just out of reach of the waves. It was important that he mustn't tread in the water, but must keep as close as possible to the receding wave. Several times he had to race to escape a stronger rush of water, then made himself stop. 'It isn't true,' he said, 'that something dreadful will happen, if I am caught.' He stood perfectly still while the water rushed in around his legs, and went out again, sucking at his feet. 'I have won,' the boy said. 'I am the strongest. I have won. Nothing dreadful happened.'

At the end of the beach, where the pebbles lay, beautifully smooth, he stopped to listen to the soft clinking of the waves washing over them, in and out, in and out, grinding them. He picked up one with the soft, red and brown blotches of the gull's egg, but on green, green like the tunnel of the wave. He cradled it in his palm, turning it slowly to see the colour, the colour of the sea in the man's eyes, imprisoned in the stone. He put it in his mouth. It tasted of the sea. If ever he had to live away from the sea, he would take a bucketful of stones to suck, to remember the time he had stood with his feet in the round pebbles and sucked the salt out of one of them.

Peter walked past the black rocks and stopped to look in the clear pools. He touched with his hand a small, round rock, completely covered with little, black horse mussels, then walked slowly up the beach to the sand-hills.

He turned once and looked out to sea where the sun

glittered. He ran down on to the sand track that led to the headland, where Mr Kent lived and worked, with the sea, the wind, and the bird sounds forever in his ears.

He stopped on the track, frowning. The dream was suddenly clear in his mind: how he went to sleep, resting on the bird's back, with his arms around its neck.

Slowly, he began the long walk to the headland. 'What did you see this morning?' Mr Kent would say. And he would reply, 'I saw the sun sparkling on the sea and the wind blowing the water on the waves. I saw some gulls working far out; and steps in the sand, that the water had cut; and stones that swirled backwards and forwards in the tide.' Mr Kent would nod his head and go on working as if he were not listening, and then:

'Nothing else?' he would say.

'I saw soldier crabs, which marched along the sand and hid themselves when I came near; and when I stopped and was quiet, and still, they came out of the sand, and marched again, as if I wasn't there. I saw a rock covered with horse mussels, so it looked like a sunflower seeded. Oh, and footprints, some going from the land, and some from the sea, and when they met they went nowhere. They belonged to the Landman and the Seaman.'

'The Landman and the Seaman, eh! What else did you see?'

The boy stopped on the track and looked around at the bushes and the sky.

'Did you see a cloud that looked like a ship?' Mr Kent would ask.

'No. But look at what I've got here.' He would take the stone out of his mouth and hold it on his palm, so that the sun would glint on its colours: 'It's something like a gull's egg.'

'It's a beautiful stone.' Mr Kent would say.

'It's for you. It's a present from me.'

'A present, eh! A present from the Landman to the Seaman.'

Peter laughed. He ran down the winding track, stripping grass-heads between his fingers, slapping boobyalla leaves, kicking with his bare feet, so the sand splayed out in front of him.

Mr Kent was not working on his boat. It stood, chocked up on beams, its ribs white and bare. Then the boy saw the hut and stopped, suddenly, staring at the open door, and near it, partly hidden, a police car.

Fearful, Peter jumped off the track. From behind a shield of bushes, he watched, listening to the voices.

A policeman walked out followed by Mr Kent, handcuffed by one wrist to a second policeman. A third man followed.

Long after the car had left, the boy crept into the man's hut. Nothing had been disturbed. The fire burned still behind a mesh screen. A loaf of bread and a hunk of butter sat on newspaper on the table with a half cup of tea.

He looked around the room, not able to believe what he had seen. He took the few steps to the bed, lay face down and wept into the man's pillow.

Only the headland remained much as it was twenty years before. They had driven, wordlessly, under the WELCOME arch down the long stretch of land behind the sand-dunes, where once had been boobyallas, coast wattle, tea-trees, banksias, low bushes harbouring birds; now tourists, holiday-ers with zinc-cream noses, caravans, shacks, boats, bottles, barbecues. Civilization had arrived.

They walked that last stretch beyond the posts where no

vehicles were allowed. At last he found where the hut had been. Scattered, burnt rubble remained. Peter said. 'He loved it here. He wouldn't have stayed with all this – with all these people.'

'You say he was supposed to have murdered his wife in Sydney?'

'Apparently he did. He was last seen there rowing a dinghy through The Heads. For years he was officially recorded as missing, believed drowned. Until my mother reported him to the police.

'She must have hated him to have done that. How did she know he was the missing murderer?'

'She didn't. She couldn't bear the thought that he and I were friends. The police wouldn't have done anything about it, probably, but when they tried to check up on his background – a Mr Kent, who had come here from God knows where –'

'What a seaman! To have come here from Sydney to Tasmania in a dinghy.'

'Seaman – yes – he was the Seaman. He called me the Landman.' Peter scuffed at the ground with the toe of his shoe as if he might find a memento to carry back with him; a round stone perhaps, something like a gull's egg, red and brown with grey blotches. But there were only bits of charred wood, stones from the chimney, and dirty grey sand, nothing else.

Peter turned then to look out over the sea. Two heads appeared, two children climbing up the rocks from the beach on to the headland. Barefooted boys with arms spread wide, jumping from rock to rock.

'Look at those kids,' he said, smiling.

THE INTERVIEW

The girl gave a shy smile and ushered him through to the room. The door clicked shut behind him.

He was trapped.

The man at the desk was writing on a pad. 'Sit down.' He looked momentarily over his glasses and pointed with his pen at a chair near the door.

Rick sat.

The man at the desk went on writing. A large man, outlined against a wide window, six floors up.

Rick could see past the man's left shoulder to some houses in Battery Point, and further over, to the edge of Mount Nelson. From the window I could see right down the river, Rick thought. If I were the boss, I'd have the desk over there. I'd have a yacht, no, a dinghy, on the river and a home on Mount Nelson. And nine bean rows would I have there and a hive –

'Your name?'

The voice startled him.

'Rick Callander – sir.' (Nearly forgot the sir.)

'Ah, yes, Callander. Here we are – Rick Callander. That's short for Richard, is it?'

'No. Just Rick – sir.'

'Age twenty-two. Bachelor of Arts.'

'Yes, sir.'

'Your school? I notice you didn't fill that in.'

'No – sir.'

'Why?'

'I didn't think it relevant – sir.'

'I see. You didn't think it relevant – sir.'

'No.'

'And why do you imagine it was on the questionnaire?'

'I don't know. I don't think it matters as long as one has the qualifications.'

'Sir.'

'Sir.'

'You don't say it easily, do you?'

'No – sir.'

'Then don't say it. Another blank. Religion.'

'Yes.'

'Yes, what?'

'You told me not to say it.'

'Not that. Religion. What about it?'

'I was not brought up in a church.'

'Nor was I, but I still have a religion.'

'Does it matter?'

'I shall ask the questions.'

'Yes, sir.' (Was he smiling?)

'Your address here is, 126 Koke Street. Is that your home address?'

'It's a flat.'

'Your flat?'

'No, a friend's.'

'Where do you live when you're at home?'

'Burnie. With my parents.'

'Why didn't you give your parents' address?'

'My parents are – I don't go home much.' (Could tell him my mother is an alcoholic.)

'Why did you do Arts?'

'I don't know. I didn't know what to do. I liked poetry.'

'You liked poetry.'

'Yes.'

'You – liked – poetry. Have you written any?'

(What has this – any of this to do with the job?) 'Yes, a few short poems.'

'Would you be prepared to do a short course in accountancy?'

'I majored in economics. Yes, I would.'

'I see. You like poetry. You majored in economics and you would be prepared to study accountancy. Would you know anything about transport?'

(Big crunch.) 'No.'

'Do you know anything about mechanics?'

(Another crunch.) 'Not really. I have an old car. I work on that.'

'You have an old car. You work on that.'

(That's what I said.)

'Why did you choose to look for a job in transport?'

(What should I say?) 'It seemed an interesting job, and I think I could do it.'

'Can you think of any other interesting jobs?'

'I would think there are lots.'

'So, this is just "a job"?'

(Silly bastard, Rick. Queen check.)

'So,' repeated the man, 'this is just another job.' It was not a question. He leaned over and pressed a buzzer. The girl reappeared. 'Direct Mr Callander to Mr Brown's office and show Mr –' he turned over a page – 'and show Mr Easton in.'

Rick turned to say thank you, but the man was already writing. He glanced at the girl. She smiled and nodded at the door. In the passage she said, 'You did well. You lasted longer than anyone yet.'

'I messed it. What is he like normally?'

'I don't know. He's the personnel manager from Sydney.

Everyone seems to be scared of him.'

'He's an idiot.' She smiled at him. Conspirators.

Mr Brown was small, his face and the backs of his hands wrinkled; yet, Rick thought, he is not old, he comes from where the sun shines all the year round, sucks all the juices out of a body. But, surprisingly, when he spoke it was as if time were his enemy. 'Rick Callander. Come in, Rick. You can join us. This is Bob Hart, Jack Cranton, Harry Mansell.' He turned, leaned over the desk and pressed a button, 'June, if Blair arrives hold him, be extra nice, I won't be long.'

Hart was a stranger to Rick; the other two he had known at university. Hart appeared to be more the comedian than a transport boss; one of those who must wear next year's fashions; his scent, not unpleasant, Rick could smell across the room. Cranton was quiet, and tough, a footballer. He could be a danger. Mansell, self-assured, loquacious, tall and blond, was wont to wear a half smile – deprecatory? Rick was never sure.

The phone. 'For you, Mr Brown – Melbourne –'

'I'll take it in your office. And dig up Blake's file –' He slid through the door.

'How did you go?' Harry Mansell asked.

Rick turned, 'Me? Oh, I messed it.'

'That's easily done. My father, he's the Q.C., told me what not to do in an interview; quite an art in interviewing and in being interviewed; essence of the thing, anticipate the answer they wish to hear, and sound sincere; absolute politeness, too, of course.'

'I tried that,' Bob Hart said, 'but he only asked me a couple of questions, mumbled his way down the card, then said I could go. Bit rude, I thought.'

'How about you, Jack?' Mansell asked.

'We got on fine. He asked me four questions. I answered the lot.'

'Right, now, you chaps!' Mr Brown had burst back into

the room. 'Where were we? Oh here you are, Easton, come in. Barry, isn't it?'

'Well,' Easton said, 'that was worse than going to the dentist.' Mr Brown matched his grin. 'We only do extractions here. Now, I've met all you chaps previously. I think you would all have a general picture of what goes on. We have chosen you for this final assessment from some forty or fifty applicants. Obviously only one of you can get the job. Who that is, is up to Mr Barry. I can say this, however, I don't know who he will choose, or why, but I would be happy with any one of you; so those of you who miss out, don't be too disappointed. Now, are there any questions?'

'Yes.' It was Harry Mansell. 'He only asked about two questions pertaining to the job. He asked me about skin-diving and surfing, but didn't seem to be concerned about – I mean I could have told him about my EDP –'

'Or your econometrics,' said Mr Brown. 'Actually I'm flattered to hear you were not asked about these things. It means I've done my job.'

'What about me?' said Hart, 'I've only been in Tasmania six months, surely –'

'Mr Brown swung around. 'Let me see: Bob Hart – matriculated Melbourne University High 1978 – Monash – missed out Stats II second year – I think Mr Barry would know all that.'

Barry Easton said, 'Will the one chosen for the job have to, say, work in the warehouse at the wharf for instance, or drive the trucks?'

'No. If you want to be a chicken farmer you don't have to learn to lay eggs. What you've got to know is why the hens lay and why they don't, and you have to learn how to produce the eggs at the lowest possible cost and sell them at the highest possible margin.'

'Then we would move from one section to another,' Carlson said, 'just to learn what goes on?'

'That's it.'

'How long would we stay in Hobart?' Mansell asked.

'Depends on circumstances: your own ability, whether someone is needed in another state; various reasons. You'd probably spend a few weeks in head office in the first year. And what about you, Rick? No questions?'

Rick was startled. 'Sorry, I was thinking.'

'We quite like people who think, provided they think along the right lines. Could we hear your thoughts?'

(Was this all a part of the assessment? What had Mansell said? 'Anticipate the answer they want to hear, and sound sincere'. His mind was a blank – all eyes, he knew, were on him, ears tuned – what should he be thinking? – it couldn't help him one bit to say –)

'Well?' Mr Brown was smiling.

'I – I was just thinking – if I missed out on this one, I might apply for a job as a heavy transport driver. Could be one step up the ladder –'

Barry Easton said, 'Not a bad idea, I know TNT encourage . . .'

'TN what!' Mr Brown swung around. But grinned. Then spoke wistfully, 'I might take you two up on that. You know, I started off as a truckie.'

There was a buzz on the intercom. Mr Brown pressed a button. 'Mr Brown, send Mr Callander along for a moment. Just a question.'

'Yes, Mr Barry.'

(Now what?)

The girl smiled as he walked towards the door. 'Come in.'

Rick blinked into the glare.

'Come over here, Mr Callander. Right around, by the window. You see all this?' He waved a hand. 'Tell me, what do you see?'

Mansell could never anticipate the answers this man wanted. There could be a thousand, but only one that would satisfy Mr Barry. What did he see? What would anyone see from a sixth floor window overlooking the Derwent? If I were an artist, Rick thought, I'd paint it: the bare masts of the fishing boats rocking arhythmically, mid-Monday morning bustle on the wharf, solitary ships ploughing up-river. Strangely, the people were small, unreal, little people. There's a title for a poem: 'The little people'.

'Well?' The voice of reality.

'Er, there's a ship on the river –'

'So, you can see the ship?'

'Yes, of course – sir.'

'What does it mean to you?'

'I'm not really up in ships. I imagine it's a freighter.'

'I see.' Mr Barry had taken his glasses off. As he turned Rick noticed the long black eyebrows actually sparkled in a shaft of sunlight.

Mr Barry leaned over the desk and pressed a button, 'Mr Brown, send Mr Mansell in, please – no, don't go, Mr Callander, just sit quietly over there – and tell me, I believe the North West Coast is very beautiful, I've never been there.'

'Oh yes. I think you would find it well worth a visit if you had time – Boat Harbour, Sisters Beach, Woolnorth, Stanley, and the bush south of the Arthur, and the mountains of course, if –'

(But there was no more time to talk with this friendly man, who was really quite – human.)

'Over here, Mr Mansell, please. Tell me, now, what do you see?' He waved again at the river.

I see, thought Mansell – something to do with transport. 'I see one of the best deep-water ports in the world,' he said seriously.

'Anything else?'

'I see,' suddenly as clear as the freighter ploughing upriver, 'I see ships loading, ships unloading, trucks lined up waiting to transport – another ship obviously heavily laden –'

'Thank you.' Mr Brown spoke without turning. Rick watched the heavy figure outlined at the window. The room was silent. Shut off from world noises. Then the voice again, bouncing off the glass. 'Congratulations, Mr Mansell.'

And turning, at last. 'You, Mr Callander. You have a problem. Perhaps – perhaps Byron could help you solve it:

> Let such forego the poet's sacred name
> Who rack their brains for lucre, not for fame.

He pressed the buzzer. 'Mr Brown, would you come here for a minute, please.'

SECOND TIME LUCKY

Tabby makes no excuses. Once he cared too but that was long ago.

Now people think because of his smell, his clothes, he's got no feelings; that he's not sensitive, he doesn't understand, or hear their insults.

He doesn't mind the children; like the two there now: Hutchin's day-boys by the look of their uniform. 'Geez, he stinks!' He looks at them so that they giggle. The others, standing a bit away, waiting for the lights to change, ignore him.

Then they're off, vying for position, over Macquarie Street to the corner of Franklin Square. Those in front are almost across before Tabby leaves the footpath.

He's slow, slow to move, slow to think. And his leg is a problem. It always aches more when it's cold. It's going to be cold tonight, gauging by the wind coming off the mountain. And the snow, already as low as the Cascades.

The policeman standing back by the steps, tall and square in his winter uniform, is camouflaged by the shadows of bare branches above him; shadows that play across his chest and face, darkening or lightening his ears, his nostrils, his hands. He could easily be another statue. But Tabby knows he's not. Tabby knows every stick, stone, statue in Franklin Square. He has studied them often in those more vivid moments between the periods of inebriety: *Edward VII The Peacemaker Rex et Imp. 1901–1910* and *The Great Navigator Rear Admiral Sir John Franklin* and that bit on the bottom:

> *Not here: the white north has thy bones: and thou heroic sailor soul*
> *art passing on thine happier voyage now towards no earthly pole*

Tabby likes that. Probably because he has been a sailor too, and would still be only for the accident. A bit like Oates in a way. But there was something friendly about going down with the ship. He could do that all right. The two of you together – you and the ship.

'You want to get in out of it tonight, Tabby.' It is the policeman who Tabby knows and can never quite forgive for finding him that night on Prowler's Road. 'You would have been dead only for me, Tabby,' the policeman had told him afterwards; as if Tabby owed him something.

Tabby nods and hunches his shoulders, but keeps his hands deep in his army greatcoat pockets, the bottle smooth and comforting, precious under the palm, the neck poking up the sleeve by his right wrist.

The harbour, as always, attracts him. He limps along the wide apron of the dock, where the small craft shelter, passing fishing boats, their decks piled high with craypots. There's something about the long, clean lines, and the sweep of the bow of another, a strange boat, that reminds him of the *Lady Cynthia*. The tall bare mast sways evenly, rhythmically, with the low swell.

Tabby stops at the seat, used in the daytime by casual visitors who come to savour the sea smells, to watch the quiet activities of boat crews arriving, preparing to sail off on some mysterious journey.

He takes a long pull at the bottle. He waits for the glow that creeps out to the fingertips. *Trina* (he reads the blue lettering on the bow) bobs gently, friendlily. From his pocket he takes a greasy, paper-wrapped parcel which he lays open on his knees, an offering from Ambrosia, the restaurant's garbage can. He pokes at it fastidiously: a chicken neck, plastic end of a salami, left over swede and potato, pieces saturated with milk or mash, a toothpick. He nibbles, then rewraps the package, pushes it back into the depths of his pocket and sucks again at the bottle.

Tabby watches them coming towards him, around the corner of the yellow-stone building. The man is tall and weather-browned like the woman. They stare at him. He watches them climb down the ladder on to the deck and disappear into the cabin. The wind whips up the surface of the water, slapping the piles and the boat's hull; lights across the dock are caught in a frenzy of shaking. Through the small, oblong cabin window there is a yellow light; inside would be warm and cosy. His leg aches; his fingers fumble for the bottle. A wind gust scrapes a newspaper across the cement and wraps itself around the leg of the bench. He reaches to gather it. It flaps like a captured bird. He releases it and watches it fly down to lie sprawled and ugly on *Trina*'s deck.

A car moves slowly along the wharf, passes him, its eyes pools of light on the black asphalt. He watches the tail-lights disappear under the trees into Salamanca Place.

A snowflake settles on his coat; another and another. They fly like soft white moths, hovering and settling, swirling, curling down on to the cabin roof, the deck. Tabby turns up his collar and pulls his hat down over his ears. The ache in his leg is easing.

The man emerges from the cabin, picks up the paper from the deck, screws it into a ball and tosses it over the side. They look directly at each other. Tabby, holding the bottle with two hands, raises it to his mouth. The man strides along the deck, snowflakes already glistening on his hair, black footmarks behind him on the decking. He turns away from the wind and pisses in a long arc on to the water. He stops with one hand on the doorlatch for a last, keen look at the watcher on the wharf. His hands shaking, Tabby raises the bottle, saluting the tall, blurred figure that rocks gently.

He drops the bottle which shatters at his feet.

The cabin door slams shut.

Lying on the bench, his knees bent to his stomach, hands tucked in pockets, Tabby is caressed and at last covered by snow. To the passer-by he could be forgotten freight, a bag of potatoes, a bundle. To the policeman who does his round of the wharves, he is something someone forgot.

Only Tabby is aware of the drama of resurrection.

The slap of water on wood is the slap of his mother's hand on ears or legs or bottom. The physical discomfort of the slats is when the woman who hates the life that has given her poverty, six hungry children and an indolent husband, has shut him in the woodshed as punishment for the night, where there are rats, spiders, and sometimes snakes.

The fuzzy warmth in his head and gut is the days with Fred and Teddy, free from home and school, exploring the sea, the boobyalla-covered dunes; lying on stomachs on the grassed plateau of The Nut, chasing the sheep, sucking the sweet stems of cocksfoot, watching Lilliputian people way down on Godfrey's Beach; the islands: Three Hummock, Robbins', Walker, Hunter; fishing boats chopping through white spray, or lying in shelter at the wharf almost directly below the sheer face of rock. But they didn't go there any more after Teddy, dare-devil Teddy, their irrepressible leader, slipped from a rock. They had watched his rag-doll, tumbling, twisting descent to the roadway, hundreds of feet below.

Fred and Tabby had pricked their fingers and sworn a pledge, shared the same woman, fought over her, and lost her when they went off to fight in a war against the Germans and the Italians on the other side of the world. And Tabby had held his mate and cried, like he had done when his mother had belted him, when the piece of shell had torn half of Freddy's head away and the blood had soaked into the desert and his shirt.

The people of Stanley had welcomed him home when the war ended and slapped him on the back and bought him beer and the policeman's kid had asked him for an autograph. They found him a job on the *Lady Cynthia*, where he stayed for twenty years until that roughest-of-all trips in September '66; the hold full, the deck stacked over high: blackwood staves for beer barrels, a pig in a crate for some King Island cocky, drums of tallow, a good-as-new BSA motorbike; and Tabby and a bloke called Charlie trying to tie things down. The pig crate went belting across the deck; both legs, arm, crate, all smashed; the pig running, steel toes uphill grappling with the slippery deck, squealing, squealing; or was it Tabby? And Charlie grabs him, before he follows the pig over the side, and drags him into the cabin.

From Stanley he was taken to Hobart, spent months in the Repat Hospital. Turned out at last on to the street, patched up, permanently incapacitated, drinking his compensation money, helped by his 'friends' who leave him with nothing but an incurable thirst for alcohol.

His 'friends', Cassidy and Macey. They had their problems. Poor old Cass – threw himself under a bus – screamed when anyone touched him. He took three weeks to die. And Macey jumping off the bridge. That was quick enough. They had dragged him from the river. Because he was a returned man the members of the RSL dropped red crepe poppies on his coffin and the President gave a short address and finished with the quote from Laurence Binyon:

67

They shall grow not old, as we that are left grow old:
Age shall not weary them, nor the years condemn.
At the going down of the sun and in the morning
We will remember them.

He was picked up eventually by Mr Crowe OBE, a respectable gentleman, with a profession of caring for dipsomaniacs by trading board and lodging in huts in the bush off Prowler's Road – including doling out grog commensurate with the amount of firewood each man cuts – for the signing over of their pension cheques.

His craving for alcohol had outstripped his capacity to work, until one dark, cold night he had broken in to Mr Crowe's office. It was the sherry which left him unconscious on the road a mile from the camp, almost stiff with cold when the policeman picked him up at two am. 'Only for me, Tabby, you would have snuffed it,' the policeman had told him.

Tabby smiles. 'Second time lucky,' he says.

Snowflakes hover, settle; soft, gentle, filling holes, corners, until the mound is even and undistinguishable.

SERMONS IN STONES

'That Shoreman woman is coming again,' I said, and dropped the letter on the table in front of him. I walked back to the stove. I was spoiling for an argument, but I never did like the eye-to-eye, close-up sort.

The picture I have of Alice Shoreman is of her standing with Brown outside her cabin, the two of them silent, looking across to Mt Cattley: past the creek lined with waratah; the button-grass plain, dotted with pandanus palms, snow gums, and small lakes; past where the dark mass of rainforest meets the big lake – the forest Brown calls the Cathedral – there they stand, unaware of what goes on around them – a religious communion.

I quite liked her the first time she came to Cattley. Then Brown set me wondering. 'Carol,' he said once, 'I was extending a track through the Cathedral today, when Alice came down from the mountain, through all that rough stuff. She got me to identify a lot of plant specimens she had collected.

'I thought you didn't like people taking cuttings,' I said.

'I don't mind people like Alice; she's too sensitive to damage the environment. The Cathedral really turned her on.'

Oh, it's beautiful, all right. But I can't get carried away, like Brown and Alice Shoreman do. When it's cold and miserable, I ache for a Melbourne northerly. And in the

69

summer there's something claustrophobic and forbidding about the rainforest that frightens me. And the mountains: it's a bit like having a favourite picture on the wall, after a while you forget to look at it.

'She's coming on the twentieth of April for two weeks,' I say, and add, I hope provocatively, 'she takes it for granted we'll have room.'

'Well, this time of year – Easter over – '

Calm, unruffled, blast him. I persist with my theme, while vigorously stoking wood into the firebox. 'The fourth year. You'd think she would be sick of the place.'

I heard him push back his chair, but I knew what he would be doing: a second cup of tea; a man of habit is my Brown. He had to reach past me to get the teapot. His arm brushed mine; I felt he wasn't aware of the currents that shoot into my brain, whenever our skins touch.

He walked back to the table. 'Aren't you going to have another cuppa, Carol?'

God! Can't I get through to him? Another cuppa. As if there was nothing wrong. Must I spell it out? I shriek at him: 'Look, I'm sick – sick – sick of that bloody woman. She's not interested in the mountain. She comes nosing around, just to see you – like a bitch on heat.'

That stopped him. I didn't want to say it. But what can you do, when he sits there like a log, cradling his tea mug, pretending – I know him well enough, now. After four years in this place, I suppose that's not to be wondered at. I know how he acts and reacts: gentle and patient, he lets me shoot off my mouth, taunts me by his silence, then when I'm starting to feel sorry or ashamed, he manages to beat me to it. 'I'm sorry,' he says. And I'm ready to forgive him anything. Let him cart me off to the bedroom if he wants; that's happened often enough.

But this time. No. I've been working up to this. This is something big. I think I've been wanting this for a long time;

even before I had the tests. Alice Shoreman coming again was about all I needed.

I heard his mug hit the table, his chair fly back. For a moment I thought he was going to strike me. I almost hoped he would.

'God Almighty! What's wrong with you?' It burst from him.

It made me feel I'd won some kind of victory. I tried to think of something to say, something biting, hurtful. A splash of porridge was festering on the stove plate. I picked up a knife to scrape it off. There was no movement behind me. I could feel his mind ticking over: what to do? what to say?

'I'd better go. I've got to clean up the track to the Cathedral.' His voice, his steps were calm, controlled. There was to be no reconciliation. Worse, no dispute. Frantically, I searched for words to hurl at him. 'Yes, go! You can't discuss anything rationally.'

'Me? What's there to discuss?'

'Nothing. Nothing. Just go. Go to your precious Cathedral. Go on. Go!' I was almost hysterical.

The shutting of the door was sharp and final. I should be rushing out after him, like the woman across the street in Hawthorn used to do, probably still does, shouting and screaming at her husband until he is out of sight. It was a joke with us neighbours; a joke, because at night, after a morning row, she would meet him full of smiles and love talk, and after a few days it would be on again.

I should have followed it up. Here, there would only be the wallabies and possums to hear, or the jays. The only guests we had had already gone off to climb Cattley.

But I must tell him about the tests. Now would be the time to do it. What do I care if he is hurt. Big, strong, dependable Brown. A god in the eyes of some who come regularly. 'Is Brown there?' And all they want is the forecast,

71

or something I can tell them. All they really want is to see him; to talk with him. To think that he, of all people, is sterile. It will crush him. Of course, I'm jumping to conclusions, a bit. I had taken it for granted it was my fault we were not having a family. I suppose women mostly do. He had helped me to think that way with his: 'Don't worry, Carol, it'll come right. We're still young. Madge was married for years before she had her first. Let's build up the business, first, before we start worrying.' Business! We never stop building it up. Each year we add another couple of cabins; more people, more animals, more birds to be fed; more tracks to make and maintain; toilets to clean; garbage to bury. At least, if we had children we'd have to employ someone to help outside.

I was worried. I'll be thirty soon, and before I know it I'll be too old. So I had the test and there was nothing wrong, which could only mean it was Brown's fault. But when I got back from Melbourne, I couldn't tell him.

I know how proud he is of his beautiful body. It is beautiful, believe me. I hold a picture of him in my mind, just after we moved into our new home – the house we built together – on one of those freezing July days, with the wind howling off the snow on Cattley. He exploded into the room, slammed the door behind him with his boot, dropped his armful of wood by the fire and stood there with a wide grin, his face and throat flushed from the wind, with the fire crackling, the flames jumping and he saying: 'Aren't we the lucky ones!' I swore then I'd love him for ever. So strong. And I do love him still, blast him. But not today.

I should have followed him out. I move over to look out the window by the back door. I know he is not there. But he is. I can hardly believe what I am seeing. He *is* there. On one knee, on the path, with his back to me, each hand resting on a wallaby's shoulder, while they nose at his shirt and his neck. He turns his head away from an exploring nose. I see

72

he is laughing. I am sick with frustration and anger.

I realize suddenly that all these years I've been blind. At least he has made up my mind for me.

He has gone now. He won't be back for four hours. If I hurry, I can catch the afternoon flight. I must hurry. Hurry. Pack what things I really want. But hurry. I've been a fool. A fool.

I always loved the mornings, even before Carol and I came here to Cattley. Partly the breakfast. My father had always insisted that we had a good breakfast. A country upbringing; always a big bowl of wholemeal porridge, eggs and bacon, toast and two cups of tea. It was one of the main reasons why I never wanted to go with Carol on her twice-yearly trips to see her mother in Melbourne; breakfast of weet-bix or corn-flakes, white bread toast and coffee; that, and the scenery: their kitchen looked out on a neighbour's brick wall.

Here at Cattley we have a view I never tire of. It's always changing. Carol and I sit looking out at it at meal times, but she rarely remarks now on the colour changes, the shades, the tricks of light. She doesn't respond as she used to to the discovery of some new plant, to the first waratah bloom, to the heavy scent of boronia, to the turning of the beech in April.

Something worries her. She returned from Melbourne looking bright and well. She seemed pleased to be back, but still I sensed something was wrong. She's often mentioned how she would love to have a family. Maybe this is part of her problem. God knows, we keep trying. I told her how Madge didn't get pregnant for years, but that didn't console her any. Perhaps she should go for tests.

We've had a quiet breakfast this morning. Carol had just thrown a letter on the table. It was from Alice Shoreman.

73

Alice has been coming every year since we started here. She is a keen climber, has a wonderful understanding of the environment and loves every part of it. I was hoping Alice and Carol would have hit it off.

Carol seemed determined to have a go at me this morning for some reason. She went on about Alice, inferring either that I have been rooting her or that Alice wants me to. All so bloody ridiculous. I exploded. Then stopped myself. Obviously there's something deeper worrying her, but there would be no point in discussing anything with her at the moment, she's too cranky. And so am I.

I stopped on the porch and put my boots on. I ripped at the lace and broke it. I told myself to calm down.

I moved out on the path and stopped. There, a bit down the track, were Ulysses and Penny, the first two wallabies we tamed. They were standing belly to belly, Ulysses' head was stretched high in the air, Penny, her front paws resting on his chest, was nuzzling his throat fur.

It's one of the reasons why I decided to live out here in the bush: the birds, the mountain, the smell of decay and the colour of new growth in the King Billy forest, sun on the spiders' webs, lichen –

They stopped their necking and turned to look at me. I squatted on the path and held out my hands. They hopped up to me to search for a titbit. Penny shoved her nose up under my chin so it tickled.

After a bit they followed me down to the workshop then lost interest. I got my tools, threw them into the ute and drove over to the lake.

There was a sharp breeze throwing little wavelets, slap and whisper, on to the beach. Soothing. Along the track I heard a wattle bird. I looked up to Cattley and saw two specks moving slowly, like ants, up the face track. I put my glasses on them. They both had jackets and day packs, one had red gaiters. I took the saw and the slasher down and went along the track towards the Cathedral. My anger was gone. It was replaced by a wanting to set things right.

I would hate to think Carol is unhappy. I must put her mind at rest about Alice Shoreman too. But I probably won't. I'm a coward at heart. I dodge confrontations. Why she should say what she said I have no idea. Could it be cancer? – hell, no! Not cancer or leukaemia! – perhaps she's, perhaps this sterility thing – they can do things about that now – can't they? – fertility drugs – which could cause problems – that woman in Hobart, wasn't it, had quadruplets –

I get a sweat up and break down through the scrub for a drink. The beach is shallow. There's a mass of small stones, washed smooth with a million years of rolling and rubbing. They crunch under my boots.

I wonder if Carol knows about this little beach. She has a thing about gathering stones, like a child; she knows nothing about them geologically; it's the colours and the shapes attract her. 'It's the feel in my heart,' she said once, and embarrassed, laughed and coloured. I've only got to picture her standing there with a stone on her palm and the colour deepening on her cheeks and throat and it makes any little tiffs we might have seem stupid and trivial. 'What's my Currawong brought home today?' I say, when I know she's been out walking. The window sill and mantelpiece are cluttered with her prizes. I find a stone I know she'll love: its form, its colours – a beauty. I drop it in my trouser's pocket.

When it's time to go back for lunch I've got everything worked out. It's wonderful what a few hours physical can do to clear the mind. I'm feeling good. It's as if I've sorted out Carol's problems too.

I leave the utility on the road and walk up through the trees. The sun splashes colours on logs and leaves.

Suddenly I get an overwhelming feeling of sadness that everyone in the world can't live in an environment like this. The beauty sucks the poison out of you. I start thinking that maybe Carol is right. This could be the place to bring up a whole mob of kids.

I'm feeling big and generous and forgiving when I walk into the kitchen.

Then I am standing in the centre of the room. Like a stump. And as dumb as one. The note on the table. Except for the hiss of the kettle on the stove, silence. Except for the clock ticking – slow – regular – endless. But the window sill – the mantelpiece – bare.

The stones have gone.

After what seems a long time I move over to the window. I don't stop to read the note. I can't. Not yet. I take the stone out of my pocket. The sun makes the colours jump. It's almost translucent. I sit it on the centre of the sill.

I move my head slowly from one side to the other to pick out different flashes of colour.

There's a magic in it. I know it's just a stone, and that it really belongs with the others down on the little beach at the lake, to wash backwards and forwards in the wind waves.

GOODBYE JASPER

For a long time I had been bugged with the thought of getting back to the family. An unidentified fear of something had stopped me. Toby had never wanted me to go. He didn't say so but I sensed it. He was my main reason for going; I had to prove to myself and my family that we were okay. More especially, I wanted my father's blessing. I felt I had let him down, and I wanted to make it right.

Looking back, it seems I never really knew my father. I liked him. Always I liked him. But I didn't know him. I wondered whether he had been happy; whether he had stuck with the family because it was the thing to do. Probably he and my mother had been happy enough in the first years of their marriage; but as long as I remember, their relationship appeared to be a constant state of making do, much, I imagined, as some people suffer an ulcer, rather than have it removed.

My mother was head of the house. She made the decisions. She had disciplined the children – 'that's no way for a bank manager's son to behave' – and my father would stare with large, vacant eyes and say nothing. I was afraid of him, I think. Probably afraid of what I didn't know about him.

There were times when my father's reserve broke down. Occasionally, he would pick one of us up and almost crush us with his big arms, then suddenly put us down again, as if he

77

were guilty of a weakness. Once, I had been involved in an accident and had been taken home. I had superficial cuts and bruises, but I must have looked a mess. When my father saw me, I noticed his look of horror, and laughed. I was immediately sorry. I had touched some sensitive part of him.

I had been christened Jasper Brown, like my father, like my grandfather. The Jasper meant that I was the first-born son. I had only ever heard of Jasper as a decorative stone, except the Romany chal in *Lavengro*. That gave me a kind of satisfaction. A vagabond. I had asked my father if he had read *Lavengro*. He had, and was really taken with it – *there's a wind on the heath, Brother*. He referred to Isopel Berners: 'now there was a woman –' and went quiet, as if he had said too much.

Several times he had surprised me by making some reference to a literary or historical figure I was learning about at school. Once I mentioned Keats, not realizing I was talking about his favourite poet; not even knowing he had a favourite poet. 'A tragedy,' he said, 'for such a man to die so young,' and quoted with unaffected enthusiasm:

> *'When I have fears that I may cease to be*
> *Before my pen has gleaned my teeming brain*
> *Before high-piled books, in charactery*
> *Hold like rich garners the full-ripened grain.*

and *Endymion*, you know that most beautiful piece of all:

> *A thing of beauty is a joy for ever . . .'*

'You and your poetry,' my mother said then, walking in to the room. As if she had prodded her finger into the mouth of a sea anemone, he had closed up, and looking at me soberly, had said, 'Keats was a great poet!'

I wished my mother would learn to keep quiet. Afterwards, I thought about that particular episode a lot. A couple of times I made oblique references to poetry, and once I asked specifically about some poet. His replies, although helpful, were not given with that enthusiasm I knew he was capable of.

I imagined he must be writing secretly. Once, when he and my mother had gone out, I had searched his room, expecting to find a suitcase packed with poems. I found nothing.

Now, after five years away, I was still not prepared to believe there had been no secret, no mystery. He was naturally a quiet, sensitive person, who was conscious of the fact that my mother had no liking for literature of any sort. Probably he had always been more interested in the arts than banking, while my mother was the reverse. She would shop around constantly for a bargain, yet I had never known her to read anything more than the *Women's Weekly*, whereas my father always had a library book out, but read only in his room at nights. His room was not my mother's room. Some years ago, he had moved out, while we were away at boarding school. It was my mother's story that she would no longer suffer his pipe smoking in her bedroom, and he had chosen to move.

Not long before we moved to Sunley there was some sort of turning point in his career. I had known nothing about Sunley, except that it was a small country town. Then some kid at school had repeated what his father was supposed to have said, 'that only morons were ever appointed manager at Sunley'. It probably was a backward step. The landed gentry there were jealous of their social order. My mother tried to salvage some self-respect in the new town, with not a lot of success, until she was able to get the word around that my father was one of the 'Western District Browns'. I must have been fifteen before I realized that 'Western District' didn't refer to Zeehan and Queenstown.

Then Uncle Ben had knocked us down a bit on the social ladder. When my grandmother died, my father had insisted that Ben should come to live with us. My mother had argued that he should be placed in a mental institution, but my father was adamant. Ben was fortyish and the gentlest person you could imagine, albeit a little boisterous at times. He smiled, or grimaced when he talked, as if he had to chew the words as they came out, 'Caaall me Beeenn!' he told me when he came to live with us, which was a bit upsetting for my mother, who didn't approve of young people being familiar with their elders. He took over the vegetable patch and transformed it into the most immaculate garden you could imagine. Sometimes in the mornings, I would see him standing there like a tree stump, just looking. I once saw a grey fantail land on his head and Ben take no notice.

My mother had finally and grudgingly learned to accept him as part of the household, but could not accept that the Bank Browns were not, and would never be, a part of that top coterie of local society. My father didn't appear to be aware of the discord going on around him. He had a workshop at Sunley, and most of his spare time was spent either in the workshop or out in the bush with one of his customers looking for some special tree.

I had one brother, Clem, and one sister, both younger than me. My sister, Tanya (born the day Tanya somebody was crowned Miss Australia) couldn't go to boarding school until she was ten because she was a bed-wetter. It was nervousness, the doctor said – and had my mother ever smacked her for it? – Of course not. Most definitely not. How absurd! – He was a young doctor, new to the town. We left him. My mother found out he was a socialist, which justified her opinion of him.

I certainly didn't love her, but I could feel sorry for my mother. She had tried hard enough to keep the family going. In most ways, I suppose, we were pretty ordinary. My mother was always harping on 'the family' as if we were trying to bust it up. 'Family life is the backbone of our social system. If the family breaks down, then, poof! so does society.' Then she would proceed to tear some neighbour to bits or to deplore the latest news of somebody down the street who had run off with another man's wife. She would shrug with her hands, head and shoulders (just like Old Artie, the grocer, when he deplored the price of coffee, knowing that he was selling on a ninety per cent markup), then she would dig up a relic of her Sunday-school training: 'Ah well, as ye sow, so shall ye reap.'

I suppose we did most of the things that normal families did in those days. We celebrated Mother's Day with white daisies. (We didn't have chrysanthemums.) On birthdays, we had a cake and candles, paper hats and sang 'Happy Birthday'. Christmas was traditional. When stockings cut out and Tanya came home from school with the news that Santa Claus and Jesus were fakes (that's when my mother really belted her for impious talk, and Tanya stopped wetting her bed and believing in God), we had presents around the tree and plum pudding with threepences and sixpences, which had to be left on our plates, washed and put away for next year. Once a sixpence was lost and my mother blamed Ben for filching it, which caused a major row. My father, who normally took no part in family arguments, surprised everyone by bouncing to the defence of his younger brother. 'No – No – No!' he said with unusual vehemence, and 'No – No – No!' louder, and hitting the table with such force that the cutlery bounced. Things happened then, as they do in a bad movie. Eyes and mouths opened wide. Ben had a fit of coughing. My father stormed out to the workshop, slamming every door as he went. Tanya giggled. Mother cried. I walked out.

But all that was years ago. This night, in the middle of June, with the rain belting down, Toby and I had arrived, and parked in the backyard of the bank premises at Sunley.

I had put off telling them about Toby. It was hard enough

in the big city, but the people in Sunley, like the people in all small towns, with their jaundiced, provincial attitudes on social behaviour, would probably condemn us. The torment of wanting to return, of not wanting to return, of wanting my father, particularly, to understand, of wanting most of all to make contact, before it was too late, had eventually pushed me this far.

We sat: engine running, lights on, rain smashing millions of glass bullets into the bonnet of the car, windscreen wipers peeling off sheet after sheet of water from the glass. The lights were on the garden. Several big cabbages stood amongst weeds, rain runnelling down their leaves. Weeds! Was Ben sick? Ben. He would be overjoyed to see me, and Toby. 'Toooobby' — I could hear him, and see his big generous smile. 'Yoouuu seeee mmmyy caaabbbaggges' — but the weeds. A cold fear grabbed me. Perhaps Ben — perhaps anything.

It had been a lifetime. Five years, but a lifetime. Toby had laughed when I had told him about leaving home. It wasn't meant to be funny. 'All because of a lousy sixpence in a Christmas pud,' Toby had said.

It must have been some sort of breakoff point, both for my father and me. I had been calm and logical about everything. I suppose I was sick of school and home. Just wanted to be free, to sort something out. I wrote a note and left. I kept in touch. Once my mother got the message that I wasn't going to university — that I wasn't going to get a job in a bank (anathema to my mind), that I was working happily as a labourer in a cool-store (even had a ticket to drive a fork-lift), that someday I would go home and see them all — our correspondence settled down to a rare and rather newsless letter. I learned that Clem had gone to Java. Tanya was working as a hairdresser in the city. Ben never got a mention. And, 'Your father spends all his spare time in his workshop.'

I reached over and touched Toby's knee. 'What do you think, shall we go and find ourselves a bed at a pub?' Toby didn't speak, just put his hand on mine. 'What d'you say? I won't mind.' He turned his head to look at me. His face looked almost translucent. 'It has stopped raining,' he said. And it had. The wipers were already starting to grab the glass.

I turned off the engine and the lights. We sat on in silence. 'They think I am hundreds of miles away,' I said. 'We can still go back.' He remained silent. The decision was to be mine. 'My father would understand,' I said, 'and Ben. My mother . . .'

We turned our heads at the same moment. Someone had walked out of the house and shut the door. 'It's my father,' I whispered. We sat perfectly still. I heard the rattling of the keys, then the door opened and he turned on the light. We could see him distinctly through the window. I was surprised how much older he looked. And he was limping. He moved out of sight, then returned, tying an apron around his waist. He stopped and appeared to look through the window, directly at us. He reached out a hand and took a piece of paper from the side of the window, stared at it for a moment, put it back and moved again out of sight.

Toby and I stayed perfectly still. His hand was pressing mine. He had such a small hand, and soft. Something was tearing at me; shrieking for me to go. We sat.

There was a whir of a motor. My father came back into view. He was holding a white board. He laid the board carefully on the bench. He screwed some adjusting knob on the side. He pressed forward with the board, leaning over the bench. Chips flew, like small white moths, and settled. He raised the board and smoothed it with his palm. It was as if he had touched me. In that instant, I knew it was what I had always craved from him, that he would touch me, lovingly, as he had touched the board. I screwed my eyes tight shut for a moment. When I opened them again I saw the shelves on the other side of the room were loaded with trays and plates and dishes and ornaments.

I eased my hand away from Toby's.

'Are you going in? Shall I go with you?'

I looked at him, but saw only his profile, outlined against the light. Where can I go? Where can we go, Toby? There is nowhere for us to go.

'They wouldn't understand,' I said.

His hand was pressing my arm. 'If you want to, Jasper, go to him.'

I didn't answer. I didn't turn on the lights. I started the car and backed down towards the street. I saw my father look around then move quickly, to press his face against the window, a black silhouette. He must have hurried to the door then.

'He's coming,' Toby said.

I turned my head away as a street light lit up the car. I crashed the gear lever into low and pressed the accelerator down hard.

I looked in the rear-vision mirror. My father was standing perfectly still under the street light, with one arm held up, as if to ward off a blow. 'Goodbye, Jasper,' I said.

I looked again when we reached the end of the block. Toby said, 'He's still there.' But I couldn't see him.

COCK-EYE-BOB

Windmill, Kim's boss at Patterson's, was typical of most of the men Kim came across out there. Certainly they were a mixture, a stringy lot, as if the sun had sucked out all their juices and left them with a hard leather skin, and a mind which expected life to be hard, rough and tough. Yet Windmill, like others Kim met, was vulnerable. The occasional glimpses of his sensitivity at first startled Kim. It seemed incongruous, but then he realized that this was the man; the other – the outer skin, the resignation to accept, the toughness – was what the climate and the land would do to anyone who dared to stay.

Nobby Hill was different.

Nobby had the pub and was fat and soft, with a belly that would be difficult to cover with a single-bed blanket. He reminded Kim of Uncle Toby, the pub keeper he had read about in a story at school.

When Kim Taggart, young, green, fresh from the Cornish village of Bude, was on his first trip to Patterson's Creek he stayed two days at Wiluna with Nobby Hill, waiting for a lift. Two days and two nights of making excuses, shoving his fingers down his throat, cursing his inability to hold his grog, and blessing the casual interruptions when station hands or the odd traveller called.

'There's always someone,' Nobby passed off the question. 'Sometimes there's two or three a week goin' north.'

Tom and Cass, two geologists, came on the third day in an open landrover on their way to Mount Essendon. After three hours driving, they had dropped him off in the middle of nowhere, where the track forked off to the left.

'Patterson's is on a bit.'

'How far?'

'Not that far. Three, four hours.'

'Thanks for the lift,' Kim said.

''S-all right. Pick out a shady tree an' have a spell while it's hot.' A shout as they moved off – 'An' go easy on the water!'

Kim had watched the vehicle, followed by a trail of red dust, finally disappearing behind a low hill. It was the first time in his life he had ever felt alone, entirely alone. But not lonely. The dust had settled. In every direction there was space, but broken by trees. And beautiful. From all he had heard from the lifts he had had since leaving Perth the week before, he had expected to find a moonscape – rocks and desert. It made him wonder whether any of them had ever been in this country. Nobby had told him there had been some rain a few weeks ago. Now the place was a flower garden. On a background of brick-red dirt were mallee gums, grey-green mulga, pink and white everlastings, rust reds, small blue succulent procumbents and spinifex, which at a distance looked like the long grass on the moors at home.

Kim had decided he would rest when he reached what Cass had said was a line of river red-gums, which beckoned from the distance. But after half an hour the gums appeared to be not much nearer. The sun was belting down now. Kim stopped, took a shirt out of his pack, threw it over his head so that the tail sheltered his neck and back. He tucked in the sleeves for a turban. He took a swig of water and set off again filled with an excitement, bordering on fear, but excitement nevertheless. He hummed bits of songs he could remember. *Come lass-es and lads, get leave of your dads, And away to the May-pole hie, For ev-'ry fair has a sweetheart there, And the fiddlers standing by.* Where the hell was he? Perhaps more important, where was he heading? And why? *Beneath it the stream gently ripples, Around it the birds love to trill, Tho' now far away, My thoughts fondly stray, To the old rustic bridge by the mill.* At least he'd have stories to tell – but they'd never be able to understand – hot meant something different back home.

Hot! It was hot all right. Pick out a shady tree, Cass had said; but he had plugged on. It was too hot to sing, hum even. But to keep his mind off the distance between him and the river red-gums, to keep up the mechanical one-foot-forward movement he tried to recall everything Nobby Hill had told him about Windmill and the country. 'He's all right,' Nobby had said. 'He calls his mills after women, but that don't make him soft like some reckon.'

'What's so special about windmills?' Kim had asked.

'Water, mate. Water. There's only one thing that keeps this place alive. Mills mean water. Mills is life. You hear that racket out there? That means my mill is working. If there wasn't no mills, there wouldn't be no water. If there wasn't no water there wouldn't be no cattle, and there wouldn't be no people; that's people of any sense, that is.'

'What about the Aborigines?'

'Them!'

'Haven't they been living on this country for thousands of years with no windmills?'

'If you want to live on lizards and roots and shit – you're not one o' *them* are yer?'

Kim had had no desire to be tossed out, which he thought Mr Nobby Hill would be capable of doing, so he turned the conversation to women, Nobby's favourite topic. He'd had an endless supply over the years. All of them had left him after a time, even though he had given them 'everything they could wish for'. Nobby had winked obscenely and patted the stomach that lolloped like a water bag on his knees.

The last one, Nobby had told him, had just disappeared. 'She walked out of the pub one night for a breath of air, and nobody's ever seen a trace of her from that day to this. As it turned out she wasn't much good. I knew she drank a lot more 'an was good for her but I didn't know how much until she was gone. I found she had cleaned up a whole case of double burnt brandy I had stashed away.'

'Oh well,' Kim had said, 'It's an ill wind . . .'

'It was more 'an an ill wind what took her.' He was leaning across the table staring hard at his guest while he filled their glasses to the top. 'More 'an an ill wind. It was a cock-eye-Bob. Them whirligigs you see around, them's nothing. Although I've seen some of them big enough – but a cock-eye-Bob! A drover came in here one day all done in and bruised. He'd been picked clean out of the saddle with one of them and after a bit, you wouldn't believe, a poddy calf was flipped up there beside him and the two of them went flying around and around, looking at each other. It took him a bit over two miles.'

Kim had been walking steadily with his eyes anywhere but on the elusive river gums. He looked now. They had come much closer, but were still hundreds of tedious steps away. And it was hotter. Another swig of water. And another. On again.

In his inebriated state at the hotel he had accepted Nobby's story of cock-eye-Bobs, but afterwards he knew it was a fiction. Or was it? Anything could happen in this strange country where, now, the river gums appeared to float in a watery haze. He had wiped his forearm across his eyes and blinked. He had looked down at the track at his feet. A solitary, white everlasting daisy had flowered on one of the wheel-tracks. The classic form, its perfection against the red, brick-dust brought him to his knees to touch the parchment petals. Carefully he pinched off a long stalk. He would carry the flower with him. Perhaps press it. Send it home to Cornwall to his mother, who loved her daisy bushes. But unlike these, the petals of hers were soft and fragile.

He must rest. Cass had told him. But he would walk to the gums. Concentrate. One step at a time. March – march – march. What's this? A whirlwind? A whirlwind? Or a cock-eye-Bob? Na, too small. Kim had stopped to watch it move slowly across the plain with its funnel mouth to the ground, sucking up bits of grass and sticks and probably grasshoppers and anything else small in its way. The shrubs and flowers and grasses were shaking and shivering as it passed, as if it were only their roots which held them down. It had to be one of Nobby's whirligigs. As it came closer he heard the whooosssshing noise. It crossed the dirt track in front of him and a twist of dust flew up to join the cranky, swirling mass of stuff up there.

Mush – mush – mush. The thought of snow and ice made it easier. Sometime, sometime, he would look up again and the trees would be there, a thousand, a hundred steps away. And perhaps a pool of water. Or a river. River red-gums. Red river-gums. Red-gums river.

Mush – mush – mush. He looked up then. The gums were close, in front of him. Certainly they were there. Dancing. Shimmering, wet and shining, because he was crying and laughing and running and stumbling.

There. He was there at last. Pick out a shady tree. Kim touched a huge trunk, red and white, green and brown, splashes of colour. And shade that reached down into the dry creek-bed.

There was shade. He had water. To drink. To splash on

his face and neck. There was shade to lie in, and now, without the weight of his pack, to float in.

Before he went to sleep, Kim had held the flower to his lips and kissed it. 'What a beautiful daisy,' his mother said. He handed the daisy to his mother and smiled. She touched his forehead with her fingertips. And his eyelids. 'Sleep now,' she said.

Before the sound, he was aware of silence, like in a quiet room when a clock stops ticking. His heart began thumping on the sand. He raised his body on his hands, listening, without breathing, waiting for the inevitable. A long way off he could hear a sound like air escaping from the valve of a tyre, a controlled hissing, closer – and louder.

Kim knew, as if Nobby was there to tell him, or had shown him a picture, that this was a cock-eye-Bob.

Over his shoulder a red cloud, wide at the top and rotating, was advancing up the creek towards him. He threw himself down to hug the ground, whimpering like a puppy, and scrabbled frantically at the sand with hands and feet. Above the din, then, he recognized a voice shouting. 'Don't worry, son. You'll be all right. Just take it easy.'

It relaxed him enough to accept that perhaps it was not the end. He felt his body leaving the ground and starting to spin, slowly at first, then faster and faster as he was whisked into the vortex. 'Steady now, son. Right. Grab my hand.' Kim felt the callouses on the strong hand holding his own, steadying him. 'There, lean back. You're right now, son.'

Kim opening his eyes and there sure enough was Windmill, leaning back against the wall of this cavity. Beside him was a tall, skinny man with a stockwhip, and a poddy calf, quietly chewing its cud. Next to it was a woman with a torn dress and long, black hair covering half her face, and a bottle of brandy in her hand, which she kept swigging.

Over his shoulder and through the red haze, Kim could see, in the distance, a windmill. It was going around with them. The rest of the country kept changing, but the mill was there all the time, just over his left shoulder, getting closer and bigger, until he could read the name, Martha, on the tail vane.

He realized then that the noise level was dropping. They were slowing down. They were either going to hit it or crash into the ground. He shut his eyes and yelled.

'Easy, son. Easy.' Windmill's voice was calm and reassuring.

Kim had waited for a bit then opened his eyes to find the face a few inches from his own. 'Windmill?'

'You know me?'

'Where are the others – the woman, the bloke, the calf?'

A dark woman came in to the room with a bowl of soup. She stopped to stare at the patient.

'He's come to,' Windmill told her. 'Give it to him.'

'Well, I never,' she said and turning to Windmill, 'I'll bring you another.'

'Don't bother,' Windmill said. 'I'll be out in a bit.'

'Who was that?' Kim asked.

'That's her – you know her.'

Kim looked around the hessian-lined walls and the square hole of a window. He swung his legs over the side of the bed. 'Where am I?'

'You're home again now, son.' Windmill was settled on the end of the bed, grinning.

'What do you mean, home? I've never been here before.'

'They reckoned it might do that to you.'

'What?'

'Make you lose your memory.'

'What happened?'

'You was out at the Forty Mile, greasin' Martha's bearings and a cock-eye-Bob spread-eagled the pair of you. I thought you was a goner this time.'

'This time? Was there some other time?'

'Don't you remember that either? In the creek with a

91

touch of the sun, that day you first come – just luck I happened t' come along.'

'When was that?'

'Twelve months back. You've been working here ever since.'

'You're kidding.'

Windmill grinned. 'Get that soup into you. In a day or two you'll be as right as ever.'

When Windmill went out Kim staggered over to have a look at the only bit of furniture in the room, apart from the bed and the bench, a battered cupboard. He opened the door and stared at the clothes stacked on shelves. On the top shelf was a tin box; in it a pile of letters to 'Dear Kim', most from his mother (he'd recognize her writing anywhere), Long-Ash Farm, Bude, with dates ranging over a period of twelve months. Under the letters was a savings bank passbook – it was his all right – an account with the Meekatharra branch of the Commonwealth Bank. He took it and the letters back to his bed and sat staring at the balance: a credit of $4286.93.

Idly, he scratched his name, Kim Taggart, in the layer of dust on the bench top. Pictures were beginning to take form, to come into focus: Perth, Wiluna, Nobby Hill, Tom and Cass, the everlasting daisy, the creek bed, Windmill – windmill – Martha – yes, he had dropped the oil can and the wrenches, grabbed the steel frame and hung on –

He looked up when Windmill opened the door. 'Another plate of soup, son?'

'No, thanks. I don't feel hungry.'

'There's nothing like a crack on the head to take away your appetite. Or a touch of the sun. She's goin' to cook you up a bit of chicken broth.'

'Windmill, what's Nobby Hill like?'

'Nobby Hill! You know Nob.' Then he shook his head. 'Nob's all right so long as you don't take any notice of what he tells you.'

'And what's a cock-eye-Bob?'

'Oh Gawd! Oh my plurry Gawd!' It was one of those rare moments when Kim was to see Windmill doubled up with laughter.

PIANIST OR POET

'Never!' said Myfanwy, with that vehemence which always made William back off in spite of his size. 'Never. Never.'

Oheee! She had the devil of a temper at times – stubborn as a pit pony. And he, a peaceable man.

It was after the accident which had claimed the life of his father, as well as twenty-two others, and from which he had escaped: by an act of God, some said.

Myfanwy Williams heard him out. His last feeble remonstrance: 'I've no fancy t'go to Australia, or anywhere. Rhondda's where I know. And Rhondda's where I'll stay.'

She had clasped her hands over her belly, feeling the life there, and had sworn that neither her husband nor the child that kicked inside her would ever be snuffed out in the blackness of the shafts that ate deep into the seams of coal, below and about the Rhondda Valley.

Not for her to wonder, like the other women of Rhondda, when they said goodbye to their menfolk each morning, whether she would ever see her man alive again. 'This place,' she said, 'is evil. The cemetery is strewn with relics of strong men who were not allowed to die a natural death.'

He had given in in the end. For the sake of peace. He had then gone about touching things with his hands. Things he might never touch again. Or see. Or smell, for God's sake.

But Myfanwy had another reason for leaving. Her mother-in-law, a bitter, remorseless woman, searching always for sour fruit to nurse her pessimism, ruled the house. Only the benevolence shown by Will and his father had made Myfanwy's life bearable. Then Mr Williams had been killed.

Myfanwy dreaded the thought of rearing her child in a house of gloom, where even to laugh seemed almost to be a sin. 'She can live with one of her daughters, Will,' she had insisted. 'This is our life, yours and mine and our child's.'

But Mrs Williams had let them go without objection; without caring, it seemed. 'We'll all come back home and see you sometime,' Will had said. And his mother had grunted and turned away, and Myfanwy had wanted to say: 'Come with us, Mam!' But could not.

Aided by luck and a compliant husband, and driven by her tenacious resolve to achieve her purpose, Myfanwy Williams and her family were moving into a small prefabricated house in the Hydro-Electric Base Camp at Gowrie Park in Tasmania.

On her first morning at Gowrie, Myfanwy woke to a sun streaming on to the cream plaster wall of her bedroom. Beside her, her husband slept. A strand of black hair had fallen over his forehead; his mouth, which was slightly open, had dribbled a wet patch on to the pillow. His features were coarse, his face meaty. He needed a shave.

She slipped out of bed and stood by the window to look over the bush to the great crag of mountain, with the sun splashing pink and gold on to its vertical pillars. It was all so much grander than the mountain over by Glencorrwg, or the Brecon Beacons, or Fforest Fawr; as grand even as Snowdon, which she and Will had seen on their honeymoon, on their way to Caernarvon.

As if to welcome her especially to her new land, two kookaburras, sitting on a gum bough, burst into a laughing duet. Myfanwy laughed too. She had seen and heard them on a film on the boat, but never in real life. It was a good omen. Any minute she could expect to see a kangaroo or a wallaby come bursting out of the bush.

'What's funny?' Will had surfaced.

'Come and look. Two kookaburras sitting on a tree. Did you hear them laughing?'

'What's the time?'

'It's morning.' But he had settled down again, pulling the blanket over his head.

Myfanwy sighed. The trouble with Will, he had no soul. He was a good husband, compared with most. He was quiet. He accepted her ideas. Hadn't he agreed to come out here? He never beat her. He was a good provider. Work, eat, sleep, and that other whenever he felt like it, especially on Saturday nights, whether or no; but as for listening to music or poetry – and he a Welshman! But Myfanwy was not complaining. He had given her Daniel, which is what she had wanted, and now Will had a secure job in a new and beautiful country.

One thing Myfanwy was certain about, little Daniel would be brought up right. She'd never forget her old teacher, Mr Rowland Davies. 'Take heed, Myfanwy Thomas,' he had told her once, 'Music and poetry are the flowers that bloom in Elysian Fields:

> Listen now, verse should be natural
> as the small tube that feeds on muck
> and grows slowly from obtuse soil
> to the white flower of immortal beauty –

that is written by a Thomas, and don't you forget it.'

And she hadn't, nor ever would, if she lived to be a hundred. Not that she could write poetry, but she loved the feel of words on her tongue. And music: more than anything in the world, she had wanted to be a singer, like her Aunt Tess, but better. 'You've a lovely voice,' people would tell her, but she knew how limited she was. Hers was a choir voice, where she could hide her deficiencies. Now her hopes lay in her son. They would climb the mountain and sit together on top of that far crag, where the sun was spilt; and she would tell him about all his Thomas relations, who sang, or played, or wrote popetry. (That Mr Dylan Thomas would have to be a relation.) Then, of course, there were the Williams: Emlyn Williams, Vaughan Williams and that American, Tennessee Williams – it would not surprise to find he came from Wales, was a relative even.

It would come out in Daniel, if she encouraged it. 'A mind must be nurtured,' Mr Davies would say, 'like a plant; feed it and water it before it will flower and bear fruit.'

Myfanwy's eyes could not devour all of the feast that this new land was spreading before her: the mountain, bulging up to soft, white clouds; the forest trees with trunks as high as six, or maybe ten houses, one on top of the other; the birds and animals that she knew lived there; the clean air without the pall of smoke; the flowering plants and trees: yellows, reds, whites, browns. Perhaps, she mused, perhaps she had found the Elysian Fields at last.

She glanced at the lump in the bed which was her husband. She was pleased he had gone to sleep again. This was her moment; a moment to think her own thoughts and dream, to ramble in a haze of possibilities: *a gold-edged invitation card for Mr and Mrs William Williams, to hear the first performance at the Sydney Opera House of that great Welsh/ Australian who has just returned from a world tour* – or – *Dr Daniel Williams, the noted organist, is to play at the Cathedral* – all their friends would be there.

Myfanwy moved silently out of the room, down the narrow passage into her son's room. She leaned over the cot. Daniel was smiling up at her. She threw back the covers. His strong legs kicked. She smiled. 'You beautiful baby. You always wake in such a good mood. Did you hear the kooka-burras, my darling?' She picked him up to carry him to the window. It was hard not to squeeze him too much. Her love was overwhelming.

She sat on a packing case. As always, she felt the almost sexual thrill as the child's mouth sought for and found the nipple. The sun shone warm on her breasts, and on the child's head. She stared out of the window at the mountain. The shaded crevices were black, against the shining silver where the sun slanted off spires of rock.

She stroked the baby's hair with the tips of her fingers. 'Daniel,' she whispered. As he drank, the boy's brown eyes glanced up to meet her own. 'Danny, the world is yours. I promise I'll help you be whatever it is you might want to be.'

He released the nipple and yawned. 'Ta!' he said; or so it sounded. She laughed and squeezed him. He fastened on to the teat again.

Myfanwy allowed herself to drift, her eyes ranging from the bush, the mountain, to the two sturdy feet with perfect toes, wiggling, until satisfied. He became still in her arms and closed his eyes. She held him cradled, with the nipple still in his mouth. She heard Will get out of bed and pad down the passage. The kookaburras were laughing again. She looked but couldn't see them. The mountain was capped with cloud now. It was soft and bubbly, as she remembered the froth on Uncle David's butter-milk.

Will had gone to the toilet. She heard him clear his throat and spit. She hoped it had gone in the bowl and not on the floor, as it sometimes did; as drips of urine often did. At least he always raised the seat. But why didn't he close the door? He seemed insensible to his animal noises, unless there was someone else in the house. She frowned. Daniel would be brought up differently.

Will was returning. She heard him stop at the doorway. She looked at him. 'How's the boy?' he asked.

'I do wish you'd shut the door when you go to the toilet.'

Will looked surprised. 'I do if there's anyone about.'

98

'Aren't we anyone?'

'What, you and Dan?'

'Daniel. Or Danny. I don't mind Danny.'

'He'll get Dan. They always do.'

She turned to look out the window.

He pressed close up against her and put his hand on her hair, stroking it gently. 'Put him down, Fanny, and come to bed with me.'

She felt his penis hardening against her shoulder. 'Oh, go away, Will. I've got a lot to do.'

'Come on.'

'Go away, please.'

'You angry about something?' he asked, backing away and dropping his hand. 'You're always bloody angry.'

'That's not fair. You know I'm not.'

'All right, but why don't you put him down if you've got so much to do. He's sound asleep. You've been sitting here this half hour or more.'

'I've been thinking.'

'What about. Have you got a problem?'

Myfanwy softened. The big goose. She looked up at him and smiled. 'No problem,' she said. 'I was just thinking about Danny.'

'What about him?'

'I always think of him growing up to be a singer or something.'

'A singer? That all. Why not? We could do with one in the pub. No one sings in the pubs out here.'

'You mean you'd like our Daniel to be a singer?'

'Of course. And that's all what you was thinking about? Our Dan being a singer?'

'Daniel.'

'All right, Daniel.'

'Or a pianist – or – or – a poet.'

'Ah, you're a one, you are, Fan. Bloody pianist, or bloody

99

poet.' He began to laugh, unreasonably, almost uncontrollably, leaning forwards with his mouth open, huh-huhhing and hissing as he did.

Myfanwy was immediately annoyed. At least, she noticed, the hardness in his pyjamas had subsided. 'What's so funny?' she snapped.

'Reminds me of somethin'. When I was a little 'un. Me Mam, she'd keep sayin' t'anybody who'd listen: "Our Will's goin' to be a pianist or a poet when he grows up, like 'is Aunt Millie or Uncle Ernie or someun."'

Myfanwy was staring at him with wide eyes. 'Your – your mam used to say that about you?'

'She did that. An' me dud used t' laugh at her. "Likely!" he'd say. "He'll be bloody miner, will our Will. Look at his muscles." And he'd push me sleeves up and make me bend me arm. She gradually gave up when she saw I was another kid like anybody.'

Myfanwy roughly put the child from her breast into the cot, so that he cried. 'Now look what you've done!' she accused.

'What's up wi' you for Christ sake? My bloody fault now, is it?'

But Myfanwy had gone. He heard her go to the toilet, slam the door, and flush the cistern. Above the hiss of water he thought he could hear her crying.

Shrugging his great shoulders, he walked down the passage to the bedroom, got back into bed and pulled the blanket up over his head.

PYRAMID OF BLOCKS

Hans Mahler went through the gate into the paddock. The cattle stopped grazing and wandered over inquisitively to stand around him, but at a safe distance. The dog stayed close by the man's leg, alert and ready for work. 'Sit, Flick!' the man said. Two steers came closer than the others, stopped and shook their woolly heads, their moist round eyes fixed on the dog. A low growl warned them to come no nearer. The man brushed a finger against the dog's ear. 'Sit!'

Big, lumbering Hans was never interested in anything apart from the land on which he had worked and lived for all his sixty-odd years. He had been a successful farmer. Some, the less generous ones perhaps, would say it was because he had worked twelve or fifteen hours a day, seven days a week on first-class land. Others would agree he was 'a born farmer', 'a natural'. He was the type cartoonists love to depict as the country yokel, coarse jowled, leaning over a gate with a straw in his mouth. How others thought of him, or portrayed his fellows in newspapers, was of no interest to Hans Mahler. His instinct, his love was for his land and how it must be cared for and nurtured. He accepted happily that there is a God of sorts, not the kind some go to churches to find, but one who works with you as long as you do the right thing by the soil, the crops and stock. He soon lets you know if you're not. Hans Mahler had an eye for symptoms of sickness.

There had been considerable change in his life in the last few years. After Nell died and Jack, their only child, married, Hans had told his son: 'The place is yours now, Jack, yours and Kate's. I'll keep the title for a while, but you run it the way you want. I'd just like to feel I can mend a fence or two, cut a bit of rubbish when I feel like it – that sort of thing.' But it hadn't worked out. He was sure she was mostly to blame. They had started off badly. Jack and Kate had been living together in town for a year or more. She had got pregnant, then not long after Nell died, and a week or two before Ronald was born, they married. They spent too much time altering the house and garden when things on the farm were crying out to be fixed. And their social life, out late at nights, dragging the child with them. It would have done her good to see how Nell had had to work when they were first married. To see Kate now with her tight trousers and painted fingernails – oh well, he hoped they were happy.

Hans shifted the weight from his right knee. The easterly weather made it ache more. And his neck too. Sometimes he could hardly lift his head off the pillow. 'Your neck all right, Father?' Kate said once. It must have been the way he had turned his head. 'Yes, thanks,' he had replied. Nell used to have some concoction made up out of cabbage and roots of some plant, which she would rub his aches with, but he didn't have any idea what it was. When he was a youngster, there was a man who used to travel around the country on a push-bike selling what he called Old Mark Liniment. That was all he did, make this stuff out of goanna oil or something and tote it around on his bike. Everybody kept a bottle on hand for sprains and bruises. It worked too, but when the old man died his secret died with him; the same with Nell.

Flick barked suddenly, a sharp, snapping bark that sent an over-inquisitive steer back-pedalling. Hans started and looked down at the dog. She glanced back at him, apologizing with her yellow eyes, and licked her mouth. She pressed against his leg. 'They look all right,' he said. He realized his eyes had unconsciously checked the briskets, loins, flanks, hair, eyes, and (if turned away from him) the tails and cods of every beast in the mob. 'Not an off-colour amongst them,' he said. 'Come on.' There was no need to tell her, she was already on her feet; she knew even before he moved; she always seemed to know what had to be done and when. 'I'm going to miss you, dog. How old are you? Twelve, thirteen – could be more.' She had a touch of mange at the butt of the tail.

The grass was lush, the place was understocked, which was better than seeing skinny cattle about. He pulled a stalk of Yorkshire fog grass and chewed the end. 'Don't let Danny chew grass, Jack.' Kate had said one day. 'Most grass saps are bad for you.' It was her way of telling him she didn't like his habit. He had been chewing grass all his life and it hadn't hurt him, had it? There was just the possibility – his aches – He tossed the stem on to the ground, and spat.

The man and his dog crossed several paddocks on to one which, recently sown, sprouted a whiskery growth, green needles of grass visible in millions when he bent right down and looked along the rows into the sun. He remembered that first time he noticed how Nell had tried not to tread on the new plants. He had laughed and shown her how he happily trod with his big feet flat on the leaves. 'It won't hurt them – do them good – consolidate the soil. Look!' And they'd watched the stems spring back up. That was a long time ago, now.

He found little problems worried him more, now he hadn't got the farm to think about. He kept thinking too much about the old days; about Nell – he missed her more and more lately – and where they had gone wrong with Jack. When he was at state school Jack had always been keen to get home and help on the farm. Then they sent him off to boarding school and afterwards to an agricultural college;

that had been Nell's idea. She had this thing about keeping up with modern trends, new technology, new ideas. She even read a lot of books herself, not about farming though. She would have hit it off a lot better with Kate than he did. Unlike Nell, Kate would read in the middle of the morning, when she hadn't even cleaned up after breakfast. In fact she seemed to take pleasure in letting him see her do it.

Nell would feel guilty if he caught her reading. Not that he did much, but he had checked the page of a book she was reading one breakfast time and found she'd read another thirty pages at lunch time.

Books and reading – no doubt there was a place for them, if you wanted to be a school teacher or something, but to be a farmer you had to have practical experience. Jack was never the same after he came back from college. There wasn't a damn thing on the farm he didn't know better about.

These book farmers. All those blokes in colleges, and the field officers, never owned a farm, didn't understand the first thing about the practical side – perhaps he should have a talk with Jack about it one day. You never see him and Kate on a Sunday walking over the paddocks to check what needs doing. Occasionally you'll find them racing from one paddock to another in the Range Rover. Yes, he'd have a talk – but it wouldn't work, she's got too much influence. There's another thing: pulling out her breast to feed the baby, in front of him, in front of anybody, no attempt to hide it.

On the far side of the property, Hans stopped to look down over the creek to Gollan's. He could see Sandra Gollan stoking a fire and hear children's voices coming from behind a bank of scrub. This was why he had really come back here. He liked Gollan; he liked the way he was struggling to make a farm out of second-class land. It was scrub country, there were some tongues of good land, which he had already cleared up and sown down, but the majority of it was hungry. Even with trace elements, it would never be much good. But Gollan was a battler and so was his wife, and if there was one thing Hans Mahler admired it was a battler.

Hans walked down the bank, crossed the creek on a log and pushed his way through the light tea-tree scrub. He saw the two girls running towards their father, who was obviously waiting for them. He scooped them up, one under each arm, two kicking, squealing bundles. Then Gollan saw him. 'Over here, Mr Mahler. You're just in time for a brew.'

The two girls were shy of the stranger and hurried back to their mother.

'A good job. You're getting it looking pretty right,' Hans told Gollan as they walked slowly across the fallow, stooping occasionally to gather a stick or root to throw into one of the piles for burning, or to shatter a clod with a boot. He liked the way they were doing it, all without any fancy equipment, and Sandra Gollan was a real worker.

He had said to Jack and Kate one day: 'There's no doubt about that girl of Gollan's,' (he could never resist a bit of a dig at his daughter-in-law) 'they'll do well, the two of them working like they do. Pity the land wasn't a bit better.'

Mostly Kate ignored him, and registered one more black mark. This time she wasn't inclined to remain quiet. 'Gipsies, the lot of them; I've seen them in town in their rags.'

Jack had supported her. 'He's a messer. When he goes broke, I'll make him an offer. I could have done in a month what has taken him years to do with his obsolete equipment.' Then he laughed. 'I even saw him the other day sowing down grass with a bag-frame thing on his stomach.'

Which had made Hans angry. 'That's a seed-basket. I'll have you know, I sowed down the whole of this property with a seed-basket.'

'That's what I mean, Dad. That was forty, fifty years ago, things alter. We're not cutting crops of oats with sickles today, or grass with horse mowers as you did a few years ago.'

Hans kicked at a sod, thinking, 'clodhoppers' the townies used to call us.

They walked over a patch of new grass, not long out of the ground. Hans stopped. 'This grass, you sowed it with a seed-basket?'

The younger man blew through his nose, shy, embarrassed. 'Yeah. Dad showed me how to use one. I didn't have a drill of any sort.'

'You've got a good strike. I sowed all of my place with a basket. Nothing I liked better than sowing down a paddock, to see the seed float and settle like moths – then waiting for it to come up – just over fifty years ago I sowed my first paddock.' Then, in case the young man thought he was soft, he spat on the ground.

'I've got a way to go then,' Gollan said and laughed, but felt a new affinity for this man who understood and admired his efforts. 'Sandra and I reckoned the country was the place to bring up kids, but –'

'You on long service?' Hans spoke the words tentatively (there was no such thing in his day). He had seen Neal Gollan working on the place on week days for a month or more.

Gollan said nothing for a moment, then looked at his neighbour. 'I wish I was,' he said. 'No, I got the bullet a few weeks ago. They've got some new machine at the factory. Stood down five of us. One month's wages and out.'

Hans felt angry. It seemed wrong that a man like Gollan should be put off for a machine. He could think of nothing to say to him. Nor would he be able to say anything to Jack or Kate when he returned. They would only tell him that it was the price of progress, that the Gollans could get another job if they really wanted one, and if they didn't, there was the dole.

Sandra Gollan had seen him when he first came out of the scrub by the creek. She had frowned. Bugger him, she thought, he's only come over for a sticky-beak, to see how long it'd be before he can buy the place. She poked fiercely at the fire. She used to get a real kick out of working here, clearing, gathering the rubbish into heaps and burning it. The kids loved working with her though they were as much nuisance as they were worth, watching them go wild, tumbling, getting covered with dirt, sleeping on a bag when they got worn out. Neal had shown her how to drive the little tractor, and look at it now – useless – waiting for money to come from God-knows-where to get a blown head gasket fixed.

But she smiled, a tired kind of smile, as she wiped the hair from her face with a forearm: 'You'll have a cup of tea with us?' she said. After all it wasn't his fault. He was always all right, different from Jack and his smaɪ.arse wife with their posh clothes, posh car, posh every-bloody-thing.

'Thanks,' he said.

She knew her old shirt was torn, and because she wasn't wearing a bra her nipples would show when she stood up; she knew her face, hands, clothes were all smudged with charcoal. She even had odd boots and Neal's cast-off trousers with two fly buttons missing and held up with green baling twine. In case he hadn't noticed, she untied the bow, pulled the string tighter and retied it. She poked at the fire so the billy shook. The two girls, playing catchings around their father's legs, burst suddenly on to the bit of rug, knocking over a pile of sandwiches she had set up on newspaper. Sandra Gollan screamed at them, so her husband looked up sharply, wondering. 'If you want to play, go and play in the paddock,' she said, and gave the youngest a stinging slap on the leg as she passed. The girl cried and rushed over to hide her head in her father's shirt. Her sister stood behind him, holding on to his belt. Gollan frowned at the fire. He put his hand down on the sobbing girl's head.

'I was just saying to Neal,' the clumsy old man said,

'you've done a lot here. It looks good.'

She had lined three mugs up on a log, and poured the steaming tea out of the billy into them. 'Sorry, I don't have any sugar. We don't take it. Milk?'

'Just as it is, thanks. It's how I like it.'

'Yes.' She answered him at last. 'You could say we've done a lot. For what? With prices as they are, we won't get much more than we paid for it eight years ago.'

'But you don't want to sell, do you?'

Ah! Now he pricks up his ears. 'Oh no, we don't want to sell. But we've got to live, haven't we? Even the tractor –' She bent over the fire unnecessarily, pushing it together so the sparks flew. Her face was flushed.

He could see the red reaching down under her right ear. He liked this young woman, there was nothing put on. She was honest.

'It looks as if we'll have to sell,' Gollan said. 'A cousin of Sandra's reckons she might be able to get me a job down in the city. Or Sandra might get a teaching job there, or both.'

'But – you're – you're country people – you're farmers. I keep telling –' The old man was flustered.

Neal Gollan looked at him and smiled. 'Thanks,' he said. 'Someday we might get back to the land. Perhaps not here, but somewhere.'

They sat on, talking about the weather, and the wallabies that were breeding like a plague, and the new grass. The two girls had recovered and were playing with some wooden blocks which Gollan had probably cut for them.

Hans watched them setting up the blocks carefully to make a pyramid, but each time, before they had completed it, the whole structure collapsed. He remembered how he had watched Jack try to build a pyramid when he was tiny. 'Do it like this, Jack,' he had said. And Nell had advised 'Let him make his mistakes, Hans, he'll learn sooner or later.' Then Sandra Gollan was on her knees beside the children.

'I'll give you a tip,' she said, brushing the blocks aside and smoothing the ground flat and thumping it. 'Always build on a solid foundation.' She stood up then and left them to it.

Hans Mahler stood too. Flick was watching him skew-ways from two yellow eyes, waiting. He swilled the rest of the tea in the cup and tossed it on the fire so it hissed. She had over-brewed it. It was bitter. 'I'd better get back,' he said.

After a bit he added, 'I hope you don't have to sell, but if you do, remember it's a good property and worth good money. Don't give it away.' He couldn't say more now.

As he moved away he heard one of the children. 'Look Mummy, we've done it.'

'Clever girls,' the mother said. 'That's beautiful.'

BERT

I had had worse than a bad run from Perth: eight lifts in two days, which included a woman trying to prove something in a Porsche 924, three or four short lifts and one with a car-load of kids which fortunately ended. They ran out of gas. Eventually I was picked up at a small place, not even on the map, called Boorabbin, between Southern Cross and Kalgoorlie.

I didn't ask him where he was going, but he had a Tasmanian number plate, which was promising.

I sat waiting for him to speak. I have found that if you greet the driver civilly and smile when you first get in the vehicle, it is not long before they speak. I quite enjoy the waiting. Mostly it is only a minute or two. Within a short time you can usually make a reasonably accurate assessment: quiet, interesting, garrulous, bigoted, irresponsible. You hope for the quiet or interesting ones. The garrulous or bigoted are usually bores; the irresponsible, dangerous; they are the reason why I don't like to declare my destination too early.

My man was on his own, driving a five-metre van. After we had gone a few kilometres I knew he wasn't garrulous, which probably meant he wasn't bigoted. My luck appeared to be in. But then he might only be going to Kalgoorlie. He hadn't said. I had noticed the inside of the car was spotless and the air was fresh, not stuffy, which probably meant he was fussy and didn't smoke. I reckoned I could do without a few smokes if that was the way he wanted it.

Without taking his eyes off the road he said, 'How far are you going?'

'Melbourne,' I said, feeling comfortable and hopeful.

He said, 'It's a long way.' Then nothing. He was possibly trying to decide whether he had to see an old aunt down at Esperance or somewhere.

I sneaked a few sidelong glances at his face and hands. The knuckles of his left hand were unnaturally large and flat. The back of his hand was covered with small scars. A line of black hairs ran down to the little finger. His face was heavy, not fat heavy, meaty. He'd be over fifty; maybe a labourer or a farmer.

I noticed, when the road was clear, how he kept looking for, or at, something on either side of the road. I wondered what there could be in this hot, arid waste, and patches of stunted gums?

'Ulini,' he said.

'Ulini?'

Worked around here once.'

'Mining?'

'No. Not mining.'

At Coolgardie we turned right on to the Esperance highway. That meant Kalgoorlie was out. He kept looking about. I supposed if he wanted, he would tell me what he used to do around those parts. Trapping dingoes? Collecting snakes for their venom? Prospecting? Cutting sandalwood?

At Widgiemooltha he stopped. 'I'm turning off here.' Hullo, I thought, he doesn't like me for some reason. But no. 'If you like you can come with me. Or you can try for another lift. I'll only be an hour or so.'

'I'll stay with you, if that's all right.' I had to find out what could be in this nothing place.

We turned down a gravel track. 'I'll show you our old

house,' he said. 'It's just down here a bit. A place called Wanaway.'

I could sense his tension. As near, I reckoned, as he'd ever get to excitement.

'All my life, as a kid, I spent here. Or nearly all. Afterwards Londonderry, for a while.'

'Londonderry? Ireland?'

'Ireland? No. Just out from Coolgardie. Just out from Burra Rock.'

'What were you doing out here?' My curiosity had won.

'Timber. My father had a contract.' He waved his arm at a patch of young gums. Their trunks were shining in a late afternoon sun, a bright copper-red. The trunks were spirally fluted. 'Gimlet,' he said.

'Gimlet. Uh huh. Your father cut those?' What the hell for?

'And me. For mine poles.' We swung around a corner and the sun splashed on his face and neck, like it had on the trunks of the gimlet gums. 'I used to know every hole in the ground for miles around these parts. I remember once we came home to find my mother just finishing painting the front door a bright red. I thought it was blood. It was the first time I had ever seen paint. She was standing there with the pot in one hand and the brush in another looking at my dad. He stared for a while then he began to laugh and my mum laughed and I laughed too, not knowing quite why, but it was good to have a laugh occasionally –'

He stopped, a bit embarrassed I guessed, so I laughed. 'It must have been funny though,' I said, 'just the door.'

We were quiet for a while, then he said, 'I wonder if it's . . .' His voice trailed off as we rounded the corner. He let the car roll to a stop and turned off the ignition. He was leaning forward with his hands gripping the steering wheel, staring in front of him and slowly shaking his head. When he spoke his voice was too loud, splitting the silence suddenly, like a voice on a two-way radio. 'It was there,' he said. 'It's gone. It seems cranky, but it's gone. You carry a thing around in your head for years – it was a good house – the garden was there – the tankstand – the dunny – it's – I'm buggered if I know –'

I almost laughed. He looked so pathetic. I wanted to pun: perhaps it has Wanaway. There with the scattered foundation stones and the chimney lay bits of fire-scarred palings and studs and twisted, rusty iron. 'It must have been burnt,' I said.

He looked at me then, as if puzzled by who the hell I was, sitting next to him. Still with that I-can't-believe-it expression he stared back at the remains of his boyhood home, got out of the car and walked (you could say walked, but stepped more) like a cat in wet grass, lifting his feet carefully over trailing plants, burnt wood, and curled up bits of iron. I sat, watching him, a bit embarrassed, as if I were intruding on some private show. I saw him stop and scuff at the dry earth. He stood up with a black saucepan in his hand, out of which he tapped the dirt by hitting it on the palm of his other hand. He turned then and strode back to the car, this time kicking his way through the undergrowth. He took his saucepan to the van, evidently to put it away. I was standing outside by a bush when he came back to stop beside me, to stare at the stone chimney, a relic of earlier, perhaps, for all I knew, happier days. 'I found a pot,' he said, 'the one my mother used to make porridge in every morning as long as I remember. I thought I'd take it home and clean it up a bit.'

I followed him back to the car. We turned on a grassed patch where he may have played ball with a sister or brother, if he had had any. We were well up the track before he spoke again. 'You get an idea in your head how things are. People too – they're always different. I imagined that when I came around the corner I'd see the old house – and the red door, still as it was. I suppose you've got to hold on to things, memories, beliefs –' He gave a half laugh and slapped the steering wheel as if by doing that he had performed a solemn, funeral rite, burying for ever, not the childhood memory of what was and always would be real, but the vision of death and decay.

An interesting bloke, I thought, sitting back comfortably in my corner, listening to him talk and laugh even, about those days of years ago.

By the time we got to Norseman we were on first-name terms: Jack and Bert. We turned on to the Eyre Highway and Bert said, 'We'll see if we can make Cocklebiddy by night.' We passed another couple of people looking for lifts. I saw him slow a bit, then go on. 'Someone will pick them up,' he mumbled, apologizing. I was pleased he didn't stop.

His wife, Nell, he told me, had to fly back from Perth because her father was dying, leaving him to drive back on his own.

I had noticed before with people who don't have much to say normally, once you get them talking about themselves, they keep going. Bert Fink was like that. Over the next four days to Melbourne I felt I got to know him almost as if I had known him all my life.

In an amateurish way I was interested in psychology, and prided myself in knowing how to get in to people, without appearing to pry. Bert Fink fascinated me. But not as much as his daughter, Bess. Bert had shown me a photo of her, that first night at Cocklebiddy. I would never have believed that a photo of a girl could have bowled me over like that one did. I know it sounds crazy, but the big black eyes became a part of my dreams, and by day they melted into pools of heat as we drove across the Nullabor. As casually as I could I'd angle the conversation back to Bess, until eventually I had found out that she had left Melbourne and was living at a place in Shepparton.

Bert Fink woke to a new day. Without looking at his watch, he knew it was a few minutes before six, but checked as he leaned over to turn off the alarm. A starling was sitting on the spouting of the house next door, facing the wind, singing. To see a flock of them in a paddock, or a long line of them on a telephone wire, they are black; this one's breast feathers shone with the metallic blues and greens of newly welded steel. Its bill was opening and shutting, its throat vibrating with the effort of singing.

The bird stopped singing, as he watched, and shat into the spouting. Every morning, Bert thought, that starling shits in the spouting, probably four or five times. There were three or more nests around the house, then the sparrows which come for a drink; that could mean forty or fifty bird shits every day. And Nell always insisted on drinking tank water every day because 'it was pure'. No point in saying anything. It would only cause problems. It always did.

He slid out from under the bed clothes and sat on the edge of the bed. He counted up to ten, stood up, took off his pyjamas and dressed. He counted, because his wife, who had been a nurse, had told him to. 'It's probably nothing much,' she had said, 'but at your age you need to take things a bit more easily. The giddiness means your brain hasn't had time to adjust.' It sounded logical enough. What's more it worked.

Bert folded his pyjamas, glanced at his wife, who, as usual, had turned over with her back to him and the window. It would be hard if anything should happen to her. She was an organizer and organized him a bit too, but he had had thirty years to get used to that. On the credit side (and there were plenty of credits) she kept a clean house; never ran out of provisions (there was always honey in the pot, tea in the caddy, butter on the dish); his clothes were always clean and ready for him to change into; she paid the rates, insurance, car registration and prepared their tax return. She was the perfect partner. All he had to do was work and he didn't mind that. If it came to a choice he knew which of the two jobs he would choose.

According to Nell there were a few families where the wife worked and the husband stayed home doing the housework. Jack Mase on the corner was one: looked after four kids, two of them not yet going to school; evidently it was nothing to see him in the supermarket with one in a pusher, another running around, into everything, and him with a trolley full of food and stuff for the house. 'Wouldn't do me,' Bert said. He had developed a habit of talking his thoughts occasionally when on his own.

In spite of the many years together, Nell and Bert had little in common, now that the children had grown up and left home. Most days they didn't see each other until late in the afternoon; their evenings were spent in front of the telly until Bert had invariably started nodding and dragged himself off to bed.

It had come as a shock to him when Nell had suddenly decided that sleeping together was not healthy and they were to have twin beds. Nell had never been able to get used to Bert's habit of keeping silent, rather than to argue a thing out, when he didn't agree. The trouble was she never quite knew whether he agreed or not, but more than likely when he said nothing she would take it he disagreed. That was one of the times; she had followed him into the bedroom and almost shouted at him: 'Well, go on, say what you're thinking.'

'I'm not thinking anything.'

'As usual,' she said and flounced out, slamming the door.

The next night he found the old double bed had gone, twin beds were installed with pink candlewick bedspreads and his pyjamas on the pillow end of the bed nearest the window. At least that was something.

He remained unsure of his expected sex role. Once, after a night out, he had come home full of booze and rolled in with her. She had accepted him, but then, as on other occasions since, he had noticed it was a cold mechanical acceptance, as if she was patiently waiting for him to get it over. It annoyed him that he had been too weak to control his sex urge; angered him to the extent that the moment the act was over, he would go back to his own bed. It was as if he had raped her. He didn't understand the ways or needs of women. For all he knew, by the time they reached forty-five or fifty, they may have had all the sex they wanted.

Making as little noise as possible, Bert went into the bathroom. He washed, shaved and brushed his thinning hair. He always showered at nights. It was only sensible, arriving home, as he did, covered with dust or dirt.

In the kitchen, he ran the hot-water tap to fill the kettle. When Nell was about, he used tank water, because she was concerned about being poisoned with copper from the hot-water tank, or flouride from the town supply.

His morning routine was simple and easy. He made a pot of tea and took a cup in to Nell. Whether she drank it or not he never knew. She would be asleep when he left it on her bedside table and he never returned before going to work. It was what he had always done. He collected the morning paper from the front verandah, which was within easy throwing distance from the footpath, then set the table.

His breakfast was three bricks of weet-bix, softened with boiling water, covered with lashings of apricot jam, and swimming in milk. This, followed by two slices of toast, thickly spread with butter and whatever jam Nell had in the dish at the time. He was no fusspot. It was a leisurely breakfast, with the paper spread on the table. He ate and read slowly, allowing ten minutes to clean his teeth and go to the toilet.

He had fallen into this routine after Bess had left home, a few months before he and Nell had left for the West in the caravan. She was only eighteen when she had gone off to live with Terry Bosisto, who had come over from Melbourne to play football. Bess was the youngest in the family and she and Bert had always been great friends. While she worked at the pub they had breakfast together and he had dropped her off on his way to work.

Now he mostly thought of her at breakfast time and wished she would meet some nice bloke, like Jack – funny that he never learned his other name. He had sounded interested in Bess, kept asking questions. And Bert kept slipping bits of information, where she worked and finally where she lived. He thought back to that last morning before she left.

'Do you mind if I go and live with Terry, Dad?' she had asked. How could he mind? If that was what she wanted, then that was it. But Nell had been bitter and angry. She had heard a lot about Bosisto, who was leaving under a cloud, for Melbourne.

Bess had gone with him, but not before Nell had warned her. 'If you go off with him, my girl, don't ever expect to come back here.'

Bert didn't believe in Providence, it was simply by chance that two weeks before he and Nell left for Perth, while he was home sick and happened to be sitting on the verandah, that the postman came with a letter for him from Bess. Bosisto had left her and she had gone off to live in a flat in Shepparton.

With Bert's reply went fifty dollars and a suggestion that after he and Nell returned from their holiday she write to him, care of the Wynyard Council. He didn't resent Nell's attitude. That was her right. She had never been able to accept the fact that young people acted differently from the puritan behaviour which her parents had instilled into her.

Bert was on his third cup of tea when he saw Ross Betts,

next door, wearing a black hat and singlet, walk down the path beside his house to collect his newspaper. Ross was as regular as Bert, just a lot later. Ross was a bachelor. He had lost his licence the previous year for drunken driving, and since then, as he too was a council employee, they had travelled together in Bert's car. Ross's breakfast was two mugs of fifty-fifty black coffee and hospital brandy.

Bert looked around. He had cleared and wiped the table, washed the few dishes and stacked them away. Everything was clean and right. Five minutes later he was backing his never-more-than-two-year-old Falcon out of the garage. Ross would be waiting on the street.

They drove a short distance down to the highway, opposite the meat works. A north-westerly wind carried the stench from the slaughterhouse directly to them. Bert wound up his window.

A motorbike passed, the girl on the pillion leaning with the driver as if she were welded to him as they weaved around cars dodging the oncoming traffic. 'Those sort look for trouble,' Ross said. 'I see in the paper that young Anderson kid got knocked. He was on a motorbike. He's critical, they reckon.'

'So I see,' said Bert.

'They got another big haul of marryanna up in New South,' Ross said.

'So I see.'

'Place called – can't think of the name – probably out in the bush a bit. Probably out near Griffis. Worked around there once. I remember . . .'

Some drivers turned their car radios on automatically. Bert had no need to with Ross beside him. Ross obviously found silences uncomfortable; at work, in the car, at the pub, wherever, if there was a man about he had to yak on. He dug up anecdotes of high adventure and hardships, love and daring, experiences he had suffered or enjoyed in most unlikely places from Bombay to Babel Island, from Turkey Creek to Townsville. Bert allowed them to wash over him, listening in part, much as he did to the radio, picking up the gist of a story then giving rein to his own ponderous thoughts, maintaining the background of prattle with an occasional 'you don't say' – 'well I never' – 'go on'.

When Ross lit up, Bert wound down his window. The blue smoke curled past his face. He pulled out the ventilator button. From the corner of his eye he saw Ross flick ash on to the floor. He pulled out the ashtray. He knew Ross would use it from then on. He did every morning; he just didn't seem to have enough sense to pull it out himself. He was what Bert's old dad used to call a 'conundrum'.

The wind smacked into the car as they drove over the ridge at Doctor's Rocks. The sea was choppy and full of froth. 'I wouldn't want to be out there on a day like this,' Bert said in a pause. 'I never was much of a sailor, and yet . . .'

'I remember once,' Ross said, 'I got this job on the coast up in New South, down near Bega, it were . . .'

Bert turned off the highway to follow the old coast road. Most mornings Ross would say, 'Why don't you keep on the highway, Bert, and turn off at Quiggans? It's gotta be a lot quicker.' And Bert would always reply, 'We'll try this way today.' Perhaps there wasn't a reason anymore, now that Bess didn't have to be dropped off at the pub – but there was something about water, the sea and Camp Creek, and the bits of shrubs all bent over by the wind, the white tips of the breakers, and that little fishing boat, lifting and dipping, determined to get out of the river, and it would.

'. . . and the trough of the waves. Jesus, you'd look down and you'd swear you'd never get out of it . . .'

Bert noticed the gardeners had planted some more shrubs along the lawn by the service station. In a few years you'd forget what it had all looked like. A three-legged dog crossing the road reminded Ross of a champion dog they'd had in Gippsland when he was a kid. 'Both his front legs with the mower at the knees – still won dog-trials with him.'

Gippsland, eh! Gippsland and Widgiemooltha. Must be all of three thousand miles apart, and here they were, the two of them, stuck down here in Tassy, within sniffing distance of the meatworks. And Wanaway – and the gums – the old house. If he hadn't seen it with his own eyes, would never have believed it. Gone! A gumtree growing where his bedroom was. At least he got the porridge pot, not that Nell would use it, but it was handy for nails in the workshop. Makes you wonder whether it's worth the candle. Build something and it goes. You keep a picture in your mind. It's a wonder your mind doesn't adjust, see things getting older, wearing out, changing – if Bess doesn't come back for twenty years, God knows what she'll find.

Even in the river it was rough. The boats tied up at the jetty moved with the slap of the water, their tall bare masts swayed haphazardly.

Bert glanced at Ross. Still talking. Some of the things he said would have to be true – no man could think up all the things he thinks up if there wasn't some truth behind them.

Bert parked his car and the two men walked over to the shed to join the few who were already there. The overseer walked across, swinging a letter by one corner. 'Another letter from your girlfriend, Bert,' he said, winking at the others.

'Thanks,' Bert said, and grinned. They could think what they liked. He would look at it at smoke-o.

The yard was filling with engine noises: graders, tractors, trucks, back-hoes. Ross moved out with the grader. The gang would be working on the detour at Cassidy's Bog. Another day on the stick. Oh well, at least he'd have plenty of time to think. Whether they gave him the job because he was good at it or because of his age, didn't matter that much.

It was a job. A man's got to do something. Only days like today, when you copped all the dust, it wasn't the best. He'd put up with it. Put up with a lot worse than that in his day. Stand there in his orange jacket and helmet with his STOP – GO stick, organizing the traffic down to a single stream, one way or the other.

'It must give you a real sense of power,' a new kid said, 'being able to stop anyone anytime, like a cop on point duty.'

'Never thought of it like that,' Bert said.

A back-hoe and a truck moved into position. Bert walked over with his stick. STOP. GO. One lot stop, the other go. As simple as that. He should have read the letter. There could be something new. Something wrong even. Perhaps she's got a new job. Or wants to come home. Then there was always the possibility that Jack . . . It was starting to burn a hole in his pocket.

STOP GO – STOP GO – Dust came away from the back-hoe in clouds; picked up by the trucks and passing cars. He had dust in his eyes, ears, mouth, nostrils, his clean clothes were already soaked in it, hardly worthwhile changing. The cars that came and went had their windows closed. The people inside were clean and fresh. Most ignored him, watched only his signal; some raised a finger; a few smiled or nodded. Today there'd be those who would say, 'I wouldn't have his job for anything', other days they'd think he was lazy, a bludger. He'd heard it all. And now, this young bloke saying, 'it must give you a sense of power'.

A log truck, followed by several cars, was approaching from one direction; from the other, hurrying to reach him first, was a Mercedes, which he recognized as belonging to that new senator. He never did like him. Bert gave the truckie the GO and heard the car skid to a stop.

As the kid said, it did give you a sense of power. It could be the Prime Minister, could be anyone, just turn your back and swing the sign to STOP and they bloody stop. The truck driver smiled and lifted a finger. Bert nodded. He waited for the cars to pass and gave the senator the GO. He sped off, skidding up the gravel, and leaving behind a pall of dust, which settled gradually all over him.

Smoke-o was slow in coming. He handed the stick to the new kid and went over to the truck to pick up his lunch.

He sat on the rim of the back-hoe wheel and took out the letter. He looked at the address. It was from Bess all right. The post mark was blurred so that he couldn't quite read the date it had been posted. With his pocket knife he slit the top of the envelope and pulled out the letter. She had written two pages, which was a lot for Bess.

'Dear Dad,' (it read)

'Everything is working out for the best over here. I've met a guy who has asked me to go with him to Perth the week after next. There's plenty of work there for the two of us, Jack says. He's a teacher and came over here on long service. He had a dream run from the West, all the way from Coolgardie to Melbourne with a man called – guess who – Bert Fink! . . .'

Thurs. 31 March (Shepparton)

Tonight is our last night here. We leave for Adelaide tomorrow and for Cocklebiddy on Saturday. By Sunday we'll be home. Today Bess had a reply to the letter she wrote to Bert last week. The big surprise backfired. He sent us fifty bucks each, wrapped in newspaper and a scrappy note: 'Good to know you're getting on well. I was hoping you would. Love Bert.'

'And you call yourself an amateur psychologist,' Bess said, and laughed so much I had to sit on her.

123

UNCLE CLARRIE IS BURIED

A Claxford funeral was a big event. Those who didn't go for some reason, usually lined up on the street, counted the cars and people, and compared the size of the cortège with others gone before. Jason and Uncle Clarrie had sat last year on the step of the hut and watched from a distance a slow funeral procession worming its way from church to cemetery. They had watched as the mourners sauntered over towards the mound of newly dug earth.

'I suppose they'll shove me in one of them holes,' Uncle Clarrie had said. 'I know where I'd sooner be though, back here in the bush somewhere, left to rot, after the cats and devils have had their fill.'

But that was not to be. Uncle Clarrie had died a natural death. He would be given a normal church funeral.

When Jason arrived at the church the seats were packed with serge-suited men, hatted women and a sprinkling of children in their Sunday best. It was understandable, Jason thought, everybody knew Uncle Clarrie by sight, if not to talk to. He had outlived all his contemporaries; but remembering what he had said last year, it did seem a bit silly, all this ceremony.

Rudi, unrecognizable in a black dress-suit, white shirt and black bow tie, stood at the door of the church nodding to his future clients as they entered. Jason was about to ease into a pew near the door when Rudi grasped his arm and directed him to a seat kept especially for him in 'the front row on the left'.

It was years since Jason had been inside a church. He dared not look around, so sat staring in front of him during the service, noting the worn blue carpet, the polished coffin on its trolley, the altar with its embroidered cloth and candlesticks, the coloured window with long-haired Jesus, His crook and flowing robe and lamb at foot. He listened to some of the things the minister was saying, but most of the time his mind was a blank.

Jason knew, by the urgent beckonings of Rudi at the end of the service, what he was expected to do. He took his place in the correct order immediately behind Uncle Clarrie's chariot for the progression out of the church.

Outside he waited with the others while Rudi organized the transferring of the coffin to the hearse, and marshalled his pall-bearers and carriers.

Jason wandered aimlessly then, searching for a tree or some place where he would not be noticed. But it was necessary that the people, congregated in groups on paths and lawns, should be able to fulfil their obligation of extending sympathy to the next-of-kin.

It was unheard of that anyone dying at Claxford should have no relatives to mourn them, so it was agreed in this instance that Jason alone could fill the role. He was searched out and his arm pumped. 'Are you his nephew from the city?' someone asked. He had mumbled a non-committal answer.

Then Rudi came with a smiling young man in tow, who was to drive him, first car behind the hearse, to the cemetery. Rudi, the general, who (so the young man told him) also dug the graves, was in control.

The minister was already standing by the mound of earth waiting for the arrival of the coffin and the crowd of mourners.

Because of the number of people present, Jason wondered whether it was to witness the first use of Rudi's machine, which was in place over the grave; whether, in fact, a funeral in Claxton always attracted such a large crowd; or whether Uncle Clarrie was regarded by the populace as an important part of their heritage.

Jason, who had taken up a position at the foot of the grave, had not long to wait before he heard the minister say:

Forasmuch as it hath pleased Almighty God . . .

And saw Rudi's foot go out to press the lever to set the coffin sinking into the bowels of the earth.

Nothing happened.

Rudi was staring at the coffin. The minister was staring at the coffin. Those near enough to see were staring at the coffin. All eyes fixed on Rudi. The minister tried again:

Forasmuch as it hath . . .

Rudi was by now on his knees pressing, even thumping the lever, his lips mouthing obscenities. He looked up frantically at the minister, who obviously had no intention of interfering with the undertaker's business. But stoic that he was, he would hold up his end as long as possible. To keep the silent but fidgeting crowd under control, he said in a flat voice, 'I shall read from the fifteenth chapter of the First Epistle of Paul the Apostle to the Corinthians . . .'

At the same moment Rudi turned to his off-sider. 'Duck over to the hearse and see if there are any straps.'

*But now is Christ risen from the dead and becomes
the first-fruits of them that slept . . .*

Jason was beginning to enjoy himself. No longer was he the star performer. Rudi, who had been wrestling with his refractory device, rose to hear the hoarse-whispered news from his off-sider. 'There ain't none there!'

126

The last enemy that hath been destroyed is death.
For he hath put all things under his feet . . .

One of the carriers whispered something to Rudi and the two men raced off to open the boot of the carrier's car.

Let us eat and drink for tomorrow we die . . .

The man snatched up a long rope and handed it to Rudi, who nodded, hugged it to his chest and hurried back to the graveside.

But there is one kind of flesh of men another flesh of beasts . . .

The carriers, now aware that the procedure familiar to them was to be followed, were, under instructions from Rudi, replacing the nickle-plated machine (which, Jason noticed, winked beautifully in the sun, and which, it appeared, Rudi would willingly have kicked), with the two smooth pieces of four-by-two, which had given such long and reliable service.

O death, where is thy sting? O grave, where is thy victory?

Rudi was on his knees, threading the rope through a handle. He passed it underneath the coffin to one of the carriers. He repeated the process with the other end of the rope through the other two handles. The carriers were standing now, taking the weight of the coffin.

Forasmuch as it hath pleased Almighty God . . .

Rudi pulled away the two four-by-twos and, losing none of his old cunning, snatched up a handful of dirt as he straightened up. 'Now,' (he spoke quietly, with his head bowed) 'let 'im go – slowly – bit more your side – steady – steady – right – down – bit more – keep 'im moving –'

We therefore commit his body to the ground,
earth to earth, ashes to ashes, dust to dust.

127

Dirt sprinkled on to the roof of the coffin. The carriers found that they had run out of rope. They followed it down until they were leaning forwards over the hole, and stopped, uncertain what to do.

With the equanimity of one whose confidence has been returned, Rudi put his foot on the loop of rope, and signalled the two on the other side to let go. Uncle Clarrie's box bumped the last short distance and settled plumb on its back.

Uncle Clarrie was buried.

NO ESCAPE

Who would have imagined that people like the Goulds would buy in next door after old Mrs Summers died? But that's what happened.

It was mainly during weekends and holidays that problems occurred: when the Gould kids ran wild across Bonnett's lawn, and Bill Gould would come over several times when he saw Jim working in the garden. 'Too much work's not good for you mate,' he'd say, and produce a bottle and a couple of glasses. What could he do? After all they were neighbours.

Then Gould's plumber's van parked as often as not out on the nature strip; and the mess of pipes up his drive; and Betty Gould, with her hair in curlers and that big laugh, forever coming over to talk at Tricia.

So the Bonnetts decided to buy a shack down the Tamar. On the morning of the day they were to look at a place at Dursley, Jim decided to erect a cartwheel Tricia had bought at an auction sale.

He heard the two Gould boys come bursting out of their house and down the drive. They skidded around the corner and stood watching him. 'What's that for, Mr Bonnett? That's a wheel.'

'Yes, that's a wheel.'

'What are you doing wiv it?'

Jim Bonnett stood up from where he was puddling

cement. 'I'm cementing it in.'

'You won't be able to move it then.'

'No.'

'Then why are you cementing it in?'

'I think it looks pretty,' the other boy said. He walked over and touched the long, wooden spokes. 'Red – blue – green – yellow –' poking his finger at each in turn.

'Don't touch,' Mr Bonnett said, 'The paint may not be dry.' Then he snatched the initiative, 'Are you boys going somewhere?' But Bill Gould was coming down the drive, head and shoulders above the shrubs and flowers where the fence used to be, his smiling eyes fixed on the gorgeous wheel. 'Come on you two, your mother's waiting for you to get ready. G'day Jim.'

'Look at Mr Bonnett's wheel, Dad, he's cementing it in.'

'I don't blame him with you two nointers about. Now off you go.'

'Are we going out in the boat, Dad?'

'If you're good.'

He watched them race back to the house. 'Such bloody energy,' he said, half to himself.

Jim Bonnett felt his neighbour watching him and wished he would go. He was not sure how best to prop the wheel so that it would stand firm while the cement set. Bill Gould was one of those who always knew. He could lay bricks, fix car engines, make bread, mend his wife's shoes, and he occasionally came out with surprising and generally useless bits of information like the gestation period of polar bears, the world's longest rivers or highest mountains. 'He is a dashed know-all,' Jim told Tricia.

Jim had two broomsticks with which he thought he may be able to prop the wheel, one on each side, provided those Gould boys didn't knock them. 'Are you going out, Bill?' Jim hoped he was.

'We're taking the kids down the river. There's a bit of

bush on the other side, belongs to a farmer I know; the kids love it.'

'Think I'll have a cup of coffee, now,' Jim said.

'You want to put your wheel up first or your cement'll go hard. How're you going to stay it?'

'Prop it?'

'With these?'

'They should be right.' Jim knew straight away they wouldn't be.

'Gawd, man! One of the kids'd only have to touch it, or a dog, or a bit of wind, it'd fall and bust your cement for sure. Hold on a minute, I'll get you something.'

'We're ready, Bill,' Betty called.

'You go,' said Jim. He'd find something stronger, better than broomsticks.

'Comin', Bet. This won't take a minute, mate. I'll be back in a sec.' And in no time he was back, hurrying with a batten and an armful of tools.

Bill drove a stake deep in the garden and nailed one end of the batten to it. 'Now, the wheel.'

'I'll roll it over.'

'You'll bust your bit of boxin'. Here, give us a go.' He grabbed the rim on each side and with no apparent effort, lifted it and sat it in the cement. 'That where you want it, Jim? Right. Hold it there, mate, while I tack the stay on. There you are, solid as a rock.'

Tricia took a rug to the front verandah and sat the baby, Edward, on it. She carried out two cups of coffee and called her husband. 'I see you've got the wheel up, Jim, doesn't it look smart?'

'Yes.'

He looked tired, she thought. 'Hard work?'

'I'm all right,' he said. 'I'm just fed up. With the Goulds in particular.'

'What have they been doing, now?'

131

'The boys asking silly questions, Bill insisting on propping the wheel his way. I would tell him to mind his own business, but he's so dashed pleasant and – and he knows everything.'

'At least when we get our shack we shall be able to get away from them,' Tricia said brightly, listening to the noise of talk and laughter and the slamming of car doors. 'It sounds as if they're on their way out now, so you'll have some peace for a while. It's not till three, is it, we have to be there?'

'So the agent said; leave here at two-thirty. But its not ours yet,' Jim was smiling, the coffee made him feel better; and the Goulds going off.

The Bonnetts watched. The Gould car appeared filled with smiling faces and waving hands. The dinghy, securely tied on the trailer, sparkled with its new coat of white paint. Bill tooted. 'Plenty of room if you wanna come with us!' shouting.

The Bonnetts smiled and waved back.

After a pleasant lunch on the back lawn, just the two of them, they left for Dursley, with time enough to stop for a while at the lookout. Yachts were splashes of colour on the river. Speedboats, with noses high, sliced the water, churning trails of white, messages of speed and power and freedom. They had tarried too long. Jim drove off down the hill, his foot on the accelerator. His tyres screeched as he rushed the too-sharp corners, but sped on. He slowed on the metal Dursley road and smiled. Tricia had been silent and, he felt, a little tense (she never liked him to speed), but now she too was smiling. He slapped the steering wheel with both hands and laughed. 'We'll get a boat with a ninety-horse merc and – and water skis. *Somewhere over the rainbow* –' he couldn't remember any more words.

She was infected by his good humour. Then saw the echidna crossing the mottled road. 'Oh Jim, look, an echidna. I've never seen one up close. Can we stop?'

They did stop but it had gone into the scrub, where there may be snakes or anything.

The river was not far below them now. The sun was shining on the water and glistening on the leaves of gum trees which were growing along the bank below the road, partly hiding shacks. On the top side of the road were some expensive houses with wide windows, grounds splendid with flowers and neat-trimmed lawns. On one block a brown body was sun-bathing on a chaise-longue; from the road there was a clear view of the white-brick house with full-front windows and the Jaguar in the double carport. The native scrub had been cleared, the lawn was dotted with exotic shrubs and bordered with rich flowering annuals. 'You can pick people who care,' Jim said. 'Some of the places are shockingly neglected.'

'And dark. Where's the place we're to look at, darl?'

'Second from the end on the right,' Jim said.

Houses, shacks, more houses; vertical, undressed board walls, cement brick, asbestos sheet; reds, blues, pastel shades; and trees.

'This must be it.'

'Waldheim,' she said. 'Isn't that what the place is called at Cradle?'

'Yes. It means bush home. What's your first impression?'

'Neglected. Better if it had been the place next door; at least they have lawns and a garden.'

'That's why it's cheap. We can clean it up.'

'Of course.'

They were walking down a winding black sand track, part overhung with native grasses and low branches. The house was further on, towards the river.

'Are you looking for me?'

They saw a man in khaki shorts coming out of a clump of bushes. He was elderly, thin, tanned by wind and sun. 'Mr Travers?' Jim said.

133

'That's right.'

'The agent made an appointment for us to see you, I believe. Bonnett.'

'The house is down here. There was a bird; I think a leaden flycatcher. You frightened it.'

'Sorry,' Jim said.

'What a mass of blossom. Isn't it pretty.' Tricia reached for a branch to smell the flowers, but released it quickly, 'Ouch!'

Mr Travers smiled, '*Busaria spinosa*. Some people call it blackthorn.' At least it seemed to make him happy.

They walked down a winding path, to a level yard shaded by tallish trees. Two hammocks were slung between trunks. Edward and I could rest here in the very hot weather, Tricia thought.

'Well, this is it.' Mr Travers opened the door. It was a long, narrow room with doors opening off it on one side. It reached to a large floor-to-ceiling window through which they could see the river. Away on the other bank, the bush gave way to green paddocks dotted with cattle and single specimen gum trees.

Suddenly, bursting into the picture, two boats in parallel, slapping wavelets leaving behind two V wakes, and towing not two but four water skiers. Yes, this view, this situation; to wake up and walk out to this in the mornings: sun streaming through the big window, sparkling on the water, cattle, green paddocks, water skiers. Jim knew immediately this was it. If there was one thing he was good at it was recognizing opportunity; he may not be as capable as Bill Gould with his hands, but hadn't he got where he was today by using his brain; making spontaneous decisions? Yes, by God, this was it! He glanced at Tricia. Her face was glowing. He nodded imperceptibly and winked.

'Noisy damn things,' Mr Travers said over his shoulders. 'Shouldn't be allowed. Should have some place set aside for that sort of thing where they can make as much noise as they want, but not here.'

Jim knew you had to humour his kind; one of the first laws he had learned as a salesman. They wouldn't be buying Travers with the house, thank goodness. He smiled at the thought. He must remember to tell Tricia his little joke, later.

'The floor seems solid,' he said, testing the spring with bent knees, a little like a lightweight wrestler, legs apart, ape arms hanging, about to spring.

'Would you like to see the rest of the house?'

He must want to get back to his bird-watching, Tricia thought. 'Do you live here on your own, Mr Travers?' she asked brightly, and then, too late, noticed the two well-worn armchairs and the woman's cardigan draped over the back of one.

'Mrs Travers is in the bush searching for orchids.'

'Orchids! In the bush, too. How lovely.'

They looked in each room and under the house where he had built a substantial workshop. A wood lathe stood near the window. Timber was lying in racks or in a jumbled heap on the floor near the back wall. 'What an excellent workshop,' Jim said, 'and the coffee table.'

'Chess.'

'You are well set up here, Mr Travers. One wonders why you would want to sell.' And realized as he said it he should not have done so.

'I told you: the noise, the people; the beach and the bush are alive with people, weekends and holidays. There's no escape.'

'Escape, from this?' Jim Bonnett was intrigued. 'Where would you go?'

'We have a place. Well, you've seen it all. The beach and the jetty are down there through the trees if you want to look.'

'We'll take it, Mr Travers,' Jim said, when they returned.

135

As they had stood on the wooden jetty jutting out from 'their' private beach into the water, which made such friendly welcoming sounds beneath them, they were joined by the common thought that this, all of this, the house and garden, the magical little path down through the trees would all be theirs. How Edward would learn to love it. And the sand, a little smutty perhaps, but still 'theirs'; the river, yes, almost the river would be theirs. They became suddenly aware of the urgency of clinching the deal. But there was no outward suggestion of excitement; a considered opinion after weighing up the proposition carefully.

They left Mr Travers in his workshop and walked up to their car, dodging the waving shrubs, the broken gum and wattle sticks.

'We'll certainly have some work to do to clean this up.'

'It's a little dark,' Tricia said, 'with all these trees.'

'Hullo,' a man was smiling at them from the block next door. They turned to him gratefully. 'Have you come to look at Traver's place?'

'Yes,' Jim said. 'We've decided to buy.'

'Good.' He stepped over the broken fence with outstretched arm. 'I'm Frank McCarthy, your next door neighbour.'

How could they not like this man with a vista of new-mown lawn behind his left shoulder?

'Drive your car down the track next on the left; we'll have a drink to celebrate. You have time?'

'Yes. Thanks a lot.'

McCarthy's place was so different from the one they'd just been in – bright colours, soft cushion comfort, television, bar. Only the view was the same. 'Why didn't Mr Travers do something about his trees?' Tricia felt safe in asking.

'Old Trav? He likes it untidy. Nice old couple, she's always poking about with binoculars or a magnifying glass.'

They need hardly talk at all with this man holding his

middle-aged chest proudly, beating out words (like a conductor, Jim was thinking), and not spilling a drop from the very full beer glass he was holding. He felt just the slightest unease, thinking of Bill Gould.

Strange that they should both be thinking the same thoughts at the same time: Tricia wondering about Myrtle, who would be dropping in for a chat – 'life is too short, dear, to allow a moment to be wasted skulking about on your own.' Very friendly, but –

'Trees, no trouble at all,' Frank McCarthy had said. He had a chainsaw; and a sense of humour if a tree should fall the wrong way. 'Enough wood to keep you going for years. Nothing like a good log fire. But work! God, work harder now with two houses to keep spick and span and half an acre of lawn to mow; keeps you fit though.' And a fist thumps the chest.

'There's a vacant block on the other side of Travers', sorry, Bonnett's, that nobody'll ever buy. Too steep and stony, only trees; cheap enough, might be worth your while getting, just for the wood.'

Frank and Myrtle were waving still when they turned on to the Dursley road. Jim and Tricia drove in silence.

It took several weeks before the deal was finalized and the Travers had moved to wherever they were going. It was on the first Saturday morning after Travers left, with the sun ricochetting off the river. Jim and Tricia woke. 'Our first morning, Jim, in our new house, we mustn't have a late start.' She slid out of bed before he could stop her, but content, he stood beside her at the window, drinking in the peace of the scenery.

He was under the shower with his ears full of soap singing 'Old Man River' when Tricia opened the bathroom door,

'Darling, Mr McCarthy just called to see if we were up. He's ready to start on our trees but said not to hurry.'

'Blast the trees! Blast Frank McCarthy!' said Jim, still with a touch of the Paul Robeson timbre, which both startled and thrilled him.

'I hope he doesn't begin yet,' Tricia said. 'It'll wake Edward. He had such a restless night.'

Jim was cross. Their first breakfast was already spoilt; and the first day, most likely, unless something went wrong, such as not being able to start the silly chainsaw. 'I'd sooner employ someone to do the work during the week while we're not here. I'm no good at cutting trees.'

When he went out to investigate he heard the sound of men's voices. Frank McCarthy was there talking with a man on the vacant block. 'You!' Jim said. He could not believe it.

'Well, bugger me,' said Bill Gould. And laughed. 'I was just tellin' Frank, we're next door neighbours in town.'

'You've bought this block?' Jim felt weak.

'Bloody oath, mate. Cheap. It'll do us with all this bush around. I'll shove a shed up here and a dunny over there. But Frank was telling me you're going to cut down the trees. You don't wanna do that. They make the place. Clean up the grass a bit. You'll spoil it if you cut 'em down.'

'I'd have them down,' said Frank McCarthy, itching for the feel of the saw. And the bit of firewood he reckoned he'd get for payment.

Oh God, there *is* no escape; now I've got two of them telling me what to do, one each side. But Jim did feel grateful to Bill Gould. Perhaps he was right. 'No, I won't cut them down yet, Frank,' he said. 'Trish thought we should leave them for a while.' He would suggest to Tricia that they plant a few more of those prickly what-you-call-em shrubs up each boundary.

'It's your place,' McCarthy said disconsonately.

'Good on ya, mate,' Bill said.

CICADAS

David was neat. Everything about him was neat: his flat, his dress, his car. And his driving.

I was feeling a little more at ease, now that my headache was going. But the heat! I would never get used to these hot Melbourne northerlies. Combine that with the hangover from the seminar, and the promise of a barbecue, and there were all the ingredients for what my wife would call a measure of melancholy.

We drove through back streets, darted along narrow lanes, presumably to miss the traffic; streets and lanes, relatively free of cars, but sprinkled with youngsters playing on roller skates, bikes, kicking footballs, and in one case a number of kids had set up a box for wickets in the centre of the road. David slowed and yelled at them and received a casual 'get stuffed' in reply.

We worked our way up from the Bay through Elsternwick and Glenhuntly. Almost, I thought, as if my host wanted to show off the dingy streets, as if the country yokel didn't know such poverty existed.

'Bloody kids,' David said once, turning a corner to find a group of them in the centre of the street surrounding two boys fighting. 'We set up gyms and places for them and they've got to use the streets.'

'Perhaps they don't like gyms and places,' I said.

I watched a young woman, garishly done up, come out from her front door, two steps on to the street. I caught her eye. She tossed her head like a fresh horse. Pride. Contempt. An old man was sitting in a wheelchair in a doorway, picking up what draught there was. In that fleeting moment I saw him as a part of the chair, a paperweight figure, part of the decaying house, part of the street of decaying houses; 'homogeneous habitations', Eve would say, or perhaps – 'a concatenation of kennels', or 'a humiliation of hovels'. She could never resist colourful alliterations.

'All these will go,' David said, waving his free hand.

'The kids?' I said, obtusely.

'The houses.'

'What then?' I smelt a possible argument, and one I felt I could handle.

'There are various propositions,' David was saying confidently, projecting himself into his dream role as the next Minister for Housing. 'The most popular is to leave the people in the area, build attractive, multi-storeyed flats and develop the remaining land for playing fields and gardens.'

'A noble concept that doesn't work.'

'Of course it works, it has been proven all over the world.'

'At what cost? When I was in England last, the Liverpool Council had developed a similar project. Within weeks, it was a three-storeyed shambles. They called it "The Pig-sty". It is still there, as far as I know. Empty.'

'Obviously something was wrong with the architecture.'

'A panel of experts found no apparent reason other than the perversity of the people whose houses had been demolished. And then, of course, there are the trees.'

'What about the trees?'

'You'd need a three-metre electric fence and guard dogs to stop them grubbing out the trees as fast as they were planted.'

'You think so?' he was obviously nettled.

'I know. The only thing these people have left is a sense of belonging, of being a part of something they know and trust; up-end that and you've got a ready-made batch of crims.'

'I understood you were some sort of Marxist, yet you'd have these people rot in these conditions.' He kept his eyes on the road and flung both hands off the wheel, and slapped them back again.

I was beginning to enjoy myself. 'On the contrary: give them work, money for food and clothes, give them education, opportunity. As a socialist, you would give them fancy, new, aseptic rooms at a cost of millions, then forget them, wash your hands . . .'

'Not quite like that,' David said, dismissing the subject.

Australians seem incapable of discussing differences of opinion rationally. They either want to fight it out physically, or treat any opposition to their point of view as so offensive as to want no further intercourse on the subject – they were the words of a visiting European sociologist. Yes, I supposed I was his interpretation of an Australian. 'You're a tiresome turd,' Eve would have accused, 'when you've got a dose of the dumps.' It was true. After all, David had been very good to me. As chairman of the writer's group he had done everything possible to make my stay in Melbourne pleasant, including putting me up in his luxury flat.

We came out on the Dandenong Road. I noticed he was exceeding the speed limit.

I was hunting for something to say when we turned off on to the Ferntree Gully Road. 'Along here a bit,' I said, 'I remember picking mushrooms and blackberries. I was just a kid. It was all farmlands then.'

David looked at me. 'You know this place?'

'My dad had a humpy down by Dandenong Creek. He worked on a farm at Wheeler's Hill.'

'Well!' David was smiling now. 'I lived off Waverley Road, not far from the R. C. College. We were almost neighbours.'

At least, I thought, we're mates again. But the prospect of

the barbecue still offered no joy. We turned into a select residential area, where trees and gardens reached down to the footpaths.

'No fences,' I said. 'Everybody must trust each other up here.'

'Of course. Don't you trust your neighbours?' But he was smiling. 'James,' he added, 'this is a fund-raising thing for the Party, but no worries, you are my guest. I have to make an appearance, but we'll go as soon as you like.'

We drove past a double line of cars, pulled in behind them and parked with the left wheels up on the nature strip. There were sounds of music, the pulse of drums, and muffled talk and laughter. Massive eucalypts reached up to the moon, above banksias and acacias.

'Who lives here? One of your blokes?'

'A very bright woman. She and her husband are both barristers. We're hoping she will be our new federal member.'

The drive was long, gravelled and weedless, sloping up to a string of coloured lights under a covered way. Faces shone like opalescent water-lillies.

David dropped two twenty dollar notes on a table and we passed through to mingle. I said, 'Don't worry about me, I'll just poke about. You get on with your socializing.'

'Sure?'

'Sure.'

I bought several raffle tickets for a trip for two to Norfolk Island, and edged down the stone steps through a crush of people, to a shaded lawn, where more people were clustered around tables laden with nuts, cheeses and savouries. An attractive girl pressed a long-stemmed glass into my hand. She held a bottle of champagne in a red napkin.

'No beer?'

'Sorry, no. Hope you don't mind. There's red or white wine.'

'Champagne'll do fine.'

A voice rasped at my elbow. 'Bloody barbecue, and no beer! Never heard of it. Somebody's supposed to be bringing a barrel but it's not here yet.'

'That's no good.'

'I don't know you, do I? What branch are you from?'

'I'm a ring-in. Staying with David Meldrin. He brought me along. Name's Jimmy Panton.'

'Uh huh. I'm Al Kowaski. I reckon you've heard of me.' And I reckoned he had never heard of Jimmy or James Panton. I only write fiction.

'Who hasn't heard of Al Kowaski?' And who would ever forget his handshake.

'So, you're with David Meldrin. He's smart, is David. Most of 'em is smart now-a-days. I'm not too sure some of 'em aren't too bloody smart. What d'you reckon?'

'You could be right.'

'Not like when Chiff was about: Chifley, Curtain, Lang, and them — and the Doc, now there was a brain,' (is he as old as that?). 'They was all smart too, but a different sort of smart — what d'you reckon?'

'You could be right.'

'Hullo, there's the beer just come.'

He left, pushing his stomach through the crowd. He was surprisingly straight for an old man, and a mountain. I pressed through the car-port, past the pits where the steak was being barbecued, past a six-metre boat on a tandem trailer, covered with a brick-red tarpaulin, on and up to a lawn that stretched back into the bush.

I stopped in the shadows. Quite alone. I looked back to the gaggle of people, attracted to the coloured lights which hung obscenely from bushes and along the terrace. The new breed, perfectly manicured, elegantly dressed, short haired, a few trim beards, ready in a flash to offer the correct profile, the *coup d'oeil*, to the candid cameras.

There was a sudden commotion at the main entrance. The pool of people rippled as heads and shoulders strained to see. Lights flashed. Yes, it was the Leader, the man himself, with his craggy face, in that light exactly as Tandberg saw him, with his wife standing dutifully to one side, while, amidst cheers and cameras, he greeted the prospective new federal member.

I saw Al on the outskirts of the crowd, apparently unconcerned by the presence of the Leader, talking with the pit attendants, who stood white-coated, white-capped, faces glistening.

What was I doing here? I was aware suddenly of the glass I was holding. It was still full. I sat it on the ground.

There was no breeze. I looked up to the heavy sky as farmers do when waiting for rain. A gum tree was leaning partly over the house. A storm could smash it on to the roof.

The music had started again. It surprised me to realize it was not recorded music. The band, I could see now, had set up below the drive: two guitars, clarinet, piano accordian and drums. Shadowy forms behind bushes were swaying to its rhythm.

I turned away from the house, the people, the music, and feeling my way, carefully fending off branches, I moved up the hill until the lights were only a dim glow, and the music the faint drumming of low notes.

I stretched out on the grass and shut my eyes. A brush possum barked, somewhere in the trees, further up the hill.

It was a dog awakened me, its tongue on my cheek, a boxer, with wide, slobbery jaws against the pale sky. I sat up and patted its head; a pup, perhaps, it was completely unafraid.

I had been asleep for almost an hour and was about to move when I was startled by a light turned on in a room of a house, no more than thirty metres below me. I had obviously strayed into someone's garden.

144

I sat with the dog, watching. The stage was set. An elderly woman was preparing for bed. Bit by bit, she undressed; slowly, methodically, dress to wardrobe, underclothes folded neatly on a chair. She reached over the bed for her night-dress; her breasts, two straps, hanging. My fingers were curled behind the dog's ears. I watched her climb into bed and turn off the light.

For a long time I stayed there; the dog sitting still, too close beside me. I eased away from its hot body, leaving my hand resting on its shoulder. Some emotion I couldn't iden-tify was churning me up. The old woman was at the core of it; or the dog perhaps. I was being told something; if only I could grasp what it was.

I stood, at last, with nothing resolved. My head was ring-ing. A ringing, a singing, as I remembered, when someone had slapped my ears. Of course! Cicadas!

I walked slowly back down the hill until I could see the crowd and hear the talk and the laughter. I stopped, feeling for the dog. I called softly. It had not come with me. The whole episode could have been a dream: the house, the woman, the dog – unreal – everything was unreal. Except the heat. The hot air was stifling.

And the cicadas. They were real. Their voices were swell-ing; filling the night.

I walked down to the edge of the lawn; an outsider watch-ing people lounging, sitting, lying in groups, in pairs, spread amongst the shrubs, in shadow or touched with coloured lights on faces and arms. There were people down there, all smiles and laughter, pleased to be with each other. Still others with cardboard plates were moving past the pits. They too were bubbling. Was I the problem? An outsider like the red-faced cooks, with long-handled prongs skewering hunks of steak, turning, dropping them on to plates, spearing fresh pieces from boxes, filling empty places on the grids. (They must soon be finished, surely to God.) Flames pitching and darting, gobbling fat; tongues, shooting out to lick chins.

Some socialist cocky must have given a beast. The supply appeared to be endless.

Is this why I was rearing vealers? For people to gorge themselves? Last month, last week, that beast, now in bits on the fire, was butting its mother's flanks, fighting, galloping over grass paddocks. It was one of those rare moments when I reached for my notebook and pencil:

> Hurry hurry young'uns, each precious
> moment closes on the time
> when you'll be herded in a stinking yard
> panic-driven down the lanes
> heel-slashing dogs
> men with electric prodders
> lead-loaded canes –

It was a thought – someday perhaps –

Al Kowaski, with his great head and neck sunk into his powerful chest and shoulders, was sitting on the trailer pole, one hand compulsively curled around an empty beer-glass. He was enjoying a private joke with one of the cooks and a girl who was replenishing sauce jugs and savoury dishes.

The cicadas were by now almost deafening. The intensity of their song swelled and throbbed with the heat as if all other sounds must cease. Indeed, it seemed they had. Never had I heard such a male choir.

As a child I caught cicadas, held them by their tissue wings, letting the light play on their jewelled ocelli, and on their under-belly where the opalescent membranes cover the sound chamber; the creepy sensation of allowing the cicada's claws to grip on to bare skin.

I remembered my father telling me of the metamorphosis from the egg to the adult, of years (perhaps three, ten, even up to seventeen) spent in darkness as a grub, finding its food from roots of trees, of its emergence as a pupa, to wait for its

146

skin to split, and *voilà*, the perfect insect. If it's female, to mate, lay eggs, begin another cycle; if it's male, to sing and sing. Just listen to them! I used to think it was sad after all those years of darkness to enjoy such a short, short period of sunlight. But they were safe in the bosom of the earth with all those delicious roots to eat. ('Hey look, I've found a wattle – be-autiful!')

They're getting louder. I wouldn't have thought that it was possible.

Then suddenly – a wall of silence.

As if there had been a conductor up there in the top of that big gum; all those cicada eyes on the baton, all those ocelli flashing colour – the majestic end to a pastoral symphony – that moment before the applause.

I held my breath. Something had to happen: one – two – three – four – five – an explosion of thunder (which must have sent my boxer leaping through the old lady's window to cringe, shivering under her bed) was followed almost immediately by a sheet of lightning, a second bolt, and the rain fell; not a few drops – a deluge.

I threw back my head and closed my eyes. The rain slashed at my face. I was soaked in a few seconds. The water was warm, purifying. I let it flow down my chest, down my back, into my shoes. I walked over to the crowd under the car-port; some were quite dry, others were in varying stages of wetness, most were smiling, or appeared to be enjoying their condition and the company, jam-packed as they were, watching the curtain of water overflowing the roof gutters.

I stood, watching the rain smash white on to the terrace, explode and join the mad race down the stone steps. The barbecue fires had finished hissing. The coals were black and sodden. The lightning persisted, the thunder exploded, not as near now, yet each flash, each clap brought squeals of delight.

People I had not seen before, and was unlikely to see

again, answered my smile with a smile. A tall youth, his shirt moulded on his slim body, and eyebrows glistening, put his hands on my shoulders and shouted in my ear: 'You're wet, however did that happen?' Clasping each other we did a quick jig.

I wished Eve were with me.

'I was looking for you,' David accused, 'looking everywhere. Where have you been?'

'I – I'm sorry, David.' I was chuckling uncontrollably.

'Sorry! Where have you been, for God's sake? What have you been doing? You're soaked.'

'Doing? I've been watching an old lady getting ready for bed. I've been talking with a strange dog. I've been writing a poem. I've been listening to . . .'

David was laughing too. 'All right, I deserved that.'

'But did you hear the cicadas, David?'

GOOD FRIDAY AND NO FISH

Seamus O'Reilly was a Roman Catholic.

It was Friday. There was no fish. Always there was fish on a Friday. If not in the fridge, then in the deep-freeze. If not in the deep-freeze, then certainly at the corner shop, which was only five minutes walk away. Except today. Today was Good Friday. The shop was shut. And anyway the Hearneys had gone off with their boat. He had seen them. So there was no fish: not in the fridge; not in the deep-freeze.

Seamus was still not organized. After all this time.

Edna had been dead for almost a year, since sometime last Easter Monday night. He would never forget that Tuesday morning. He had wakened as he mostly did, facing the window, his eyes on the magnolia tree. In that first moment he had been held motionless, petrified, sure that something dreadful had happened. The leaves of the magnolia were quite still. There was no sound of any sort; no traffic noises – no breathing. Seamus had turned slowly, fearfully, knowing what he would find. Edna lay, her mouth, her eyes, slightly

149

open; her book, where it had fallen by her pillow. She was quite cold, and stiff. She was dead, of course.

Oh, dear! If only he had remembered. The shop shut, and not a skerrick of fish in the house; not even a parrot head for the cat. That was remiss of him. He laughed then; without mirth. He must be going crazy. The cat, too, was dead. It had been dead for a month or more.

Seamus shuddered still when he recalled that he had spent the whole night back to back with a corpse. At first he had felt a confusion of emotions: sadness, physical pain, horror, fear. He had always relied so completely upon her. She had been so sure, so knowing. He had felt secure: 'Edna, what do you think?' – 'Edna, should I . . .?' – 'Edna?'

And shame. That was another of the emotions he had experienced as he looked down at Edna that Tuesday morning. Shame and guilt: that he had felt a surging of desire early in the night; he had run his hand up her thigh and because she had made no response he had, as always, quickly withdrawn his hand, resigned himself and turned to sleep, back to back. And all the time –

Now there was no fish. They had been married – how long? – forty, forty-one years, and never once had they gone without fish on a Friday. Not that there was any great religious significance about it. Perhaps nothing more than a habit. 'We are creatures of habit,' Edna had said it so often; one of her clichés. In fact, that, in itself, was a habit: 'Don't expect me to change at my age, I am a creature of habit,' Edna would say. And because she said a thing Seamus accepted it. That, too, was habit.

And now, no fish. Not that he cared for fish. He would have been quite content without it. But the breaking of a habit, that was the scary part. Edna had always insisted on fish on Fridays. And she was not a Roman Catholic. Perhaps that was her big compromise.

Then there were the chairs. They had each had their own chair in the library. The library had always been the lumber room as long as Seamus remembered, until his mother and father had gone to live in the Retirement Village, then Edna had included that room in her upturning, reorganizing of the place.

The lumber had gone (most of it to Saint Vinnies'), the walls of the tiny room had been fitted with shelves for books (the ordinary, rather tatty ones behind the door, the Reader's Club books and the set of Chambers' the family had had since he was a child, on the facing wall).

Between the window and the door (to catch the draughts in summer) were two Louis XVI armchairs, one on each side of the rosewood, inlaid chess table, and facing the only other furnishings in the room, the electric imitation-woodfire and the television set.

Each night after tea, they would go to the library to watch television, or to read. Sometimes they would draw their chairs up to the table to play rummy or crib. That was Seamus's compromise. Chess was really his game, but the set, a beautifully turned moss agate wedding present, had remained in the drawer, undisturbed, on Edna's side of the table.

For any serious discussion they would sit facing each other

across the low table. 'A communion of saints,' Edna had once said. Her sense of humour. Seamus remembered clearly several crises when he had been quite determined that he would be absolutely unyielding in his resolve to be, to do, to have, or not to have, as the case might be. Yet each time she had overwhelmed him, not just by her logic, which mostly was faultless, but by the strength of the conviction that she did, after all, know.

Ah, why had he not thought of it? There could be a tin of salmon in the cupboard. Salad with salmon. Or pilchards. Of course! That would be a pleasant change. It had been ages since he had had pilchards. Edna had always kept them on hand for when she drove him out in to the country for an occasional picnic.

Those were the days. Except, he remembered, that time when they had settled beside a river bank and had been surprised by a mob of cattle that had galloped up from no-where, and would, no doubt, have trodden them into the ground, had not Edna swept up the blanket with all their gear and urged him, with her, into and across the river. That was one of the few times when Seamus had wondered if Edna had made the right decision. They had stood on the opposite bank, cold and dripping, watching the fat, red bodies jostling each other to get to the water where they lined up to drink. They appeared so quiet and gentle, with long necks stretched out and lips kissing the surface, not even making a ripple. And their reflections. He remembered, then, even in his discomfort, wishing that he had learnt to paint.

Seamus stood at the door of the library looking at the

scene where he and Edna had spent so many evenings together. It was strange, now that he thought about it, that he had never sat in Edna's chair. He had never even thought about it. He had not used the library after Edna's death, except to take or replace a book, which he read, either sitting in the kitchen or in bed. And to clean it, of course, vacuuming and dusting, just as she had always done. But to sit in her chair. When she was alive it would have been unthinkable, just as it would have been for him to walk into the bathroom while she was showering. Right from the beginning, there had been no need for Edna to lock the door.

Seamus thought it must have been because he was naturally timid. It had been mutually accepted, when they were married, never to see each other naked, front on. And anything that happened in bed had always to be performed with the light out. Edna had mentioned at the outset that it would be disgusting to have it otherwise. Seamus accepted that, as he had always accepted everything that Edna had told him. Thinking about it, the only female private parts he had ever seen was on the fold-out, flesh-coloured diagram in the encyclopaedia, which, at first, he had often secretly studied, until, one day, he had blushed to find that both it and the male figure had been removed: a discovery which had filled him with an extraordinary sense of guilt, and about which he could, of course, say nothing.

He had always had the feeling that he had missed out on many things in life but never, until this moment, standing in the library doorway, had he considered just how much he had been denied.

He would do something about it. He didn't quite know what or how. It was a bit scary. But exciting.

Even as the thought struck him, he began moving from the door around the chess table – five steps and he was facing Edna's empty chair. Hesitating, only for a brief moment, before sitting heavily. He laughed. Surely it was some kind of victory. He bounced up and down and remembered being beaten, as a child, for jumping on chairs. But no one would beat him now. He stood on the seat, and holding the back of the chair, jumped and jumped, until he was breathless.

Another childhood memory came bounding into his head. He had been staying on his uncle's farm when he was about eight or nine. Uncle had let a calf out of the barn, where it had been in the semi-dark interior for several weeks, knowing only the soft straw and the twice-a-day feeds of warm cow's milk in a bucket. Then it had been coaxed outside. 'Watch 'im,' Uncle had said, his face brimming over with knowing. Dazed by sunlight, uncertain of the strange, new world of space, green grass and solid earth, and smells that weren't of urine- and dung-soaked straw, the calf had accepted Uncle's prodding and pushing and shoo-shooing, until it was aware that it had entered a new world waiting to be explored. Hesitant, stumbling at first, it took off, galloping full pelt down the paddock, its tail a vertical mast, with the switch streaming like a flag, as if Uncle had combed it especially.

They had watched it prop suddenly and let out a deep staccato bawl, before shooting off in some new direction. Up and down, backwards and forwards, it skidded at last to a four-footed prop-stop in front of them, the man and the boy, laughing like jackasses at the barn door. Seamus had bent down to hug the hot, glossy neck, and to feel the belly heaving.

Seamus O'Reilly made his own calfy bellow, which really sounded nothing like a calf, but it pleased him nevertheless. He jumped down off Edna's chair, grasped the back and tipped it sideways. He tossed the chess table so that it lay on its back with its legs in the air. In passing, he threw his own chair over on its side and marched out of the room, down the hall, into the kitchen.

He stopped in the centre of the room, marvelling at the cleanliness, the tidiness, the order; all exactly as Edna had kept it. He lifted the side of the table so that the cup and saucer, the sugar bowl and the milk jug, all neatly placed, ready for his morning tea, crashed on to the floor.

Crunching over the spilt sugar and broken glass, Seamus searched at the back of the food cupboard, and there: one tin of sardines, one tin of salmon, and two tins of pilchards, (which Edna must have purchased at least one year previously).

One after the other, he opened them all, tipped the contents into the empty milk carton, ready for the compost heap, threw the tins into the garbage, and after carefully washing and drying his hands (which he was prompted to examine critically, and admire), he walked down the hall to take his hat and walking stick from the hall-stand.

His wife's portrait was hanging on the wall opposite. In the mirror Seamus caught her rather serious expression appraising him critically over his right shoulder. He held her eyes with his, raised his hat and smiled.

ALSO FROM McPHEE GRIBBLE/PENGUIN

WHERE'S MORNING GONE?
Barney Roberts

'This morning he was early.

He slid out of bed on to the mat, picked up the bundle of clothes his mother had put ready for him on the box and hurried out to the kitchen on his toes. The board floors were cold. The linoleum in the kitchen was colder.

He threw his clothes on the floor and stood on them. He opened the fire-box and stood, soaking in the flush of warmth on his back and belly. He dressed then, cut himself a slice of bread, toasted it and spread it with pork dripping.

He pulled on his boots, walked out on to the verandah and stood on the back step looking down over the garden to the river flats.

The sun had just poked over the dip of Medwin's Hill. A heavy frost covered everything except for the brown willows following the course of the river.'

Barney Roberts has lived all his life where his parents lived most of theirs – on a farm in northern Tasmania. He is a plain writer of plain truths – the kind that leave a longing for the small world he calls up.

COMMON KNOWLEDGE
An illustrated folk history of Ireland

Olive Sharkey

There was no end to the ingenuity and resourcefulness of our Celtic forebears, who invented ways to farm, garden and housekeep all their own. Many of these were transported to Australia and have left their traces in our countryside to the present day.

Common Knowledge is a loving but unsentimental evocation of Irish folk history from 1800 to the 1930s.

'It will please the romantic and the fact-grubber equally well.'
Dinny O'Hearn